WHAT YOU PROMISED

ANYTHING FOR LOVE - BOOK 4

ADELE CLEE

Cover designed by **Jay Aheer**

CHAPTER 1

*M*atthew Chandler stared at the petite golden-haired lady standing in front of him. Her perfect bow-shaped lips formed a delightful pout. Her wide blue eyes gazed up as if he were a wise scholar with the answers to all life's weird and wonderful mysteries.

He had seen desire flash in many a woman's eye, but he had never seen hope. It was certainly a novelty.

"Do you want to marry Lord Morford?" Matthew gestured to his friend whose persistent shuffling showed a desperate need to find another solution to their impending problem.

Something had to be done.

In a matter of minutes, the matrons heading their way would enter the secluded corner of Lord Holbrook's garden. One could only imagine the look of horror on the ladies' faces upon discovering a dishevelled maiden hiding behind the shrubbery with two rogues.

"No." Miss Smythe glanced at Tristan's handsome countenance, her gaze passing over him as one would a faded bonnet in a shop window. "I do not want to marry Lord Morford. But what else can I do?"

Tristan rubbed the back of his neck. "My mother knows how to execute a cunning plan and lured us both out here. She insists I wed Miss Smythe. Thank you for alerting us to the danger, Chandler, but I see no other option."

With a raised brow, Matthew considered the torn bodice of Miss Smythe's gown. A frustrated groan left his lips. Regardless of the lady's wishes, Tristan would make her an offer of marriage. He would not let an innocent woman suffer the shame of a ruined reputation.

"May I offer another suggestion?" Matthew's gaze fell to the soft curve of Miss Smythe's breasts. "If you do not want to marry Lord Morford, then perhaps you might marry me." The words tumbled from his mouth with surprising ease.

Tristan sucked in a sharp breath. "What the blazes? We are trying to salvage the lady's reputation, not ruin it beyond redemption."

Matthew smiled as Miss Smythe's curious gaze drifted over the breadth of his chest. She bit down on her bottom lip, and devil take him, desire flashed in her eyes.

How intriguing.

This timid little creature might prove far more entertaining than he'd suspected.

"Is ... is that an offer, sir?" She batted her long lashes more times than he cared to count.

From her flirtatious tone, he knew he'd captured her interest. Perhaps the evening would not be a complete disaster. And if his information proved correct, the lady had a decent enough dowry to ease his financial burden.

"It is," he replied with an air of confidence.

Tristan inhaled deeply. "I can't let you do that."

Matthew shrugged. "It is not your decision to make." Indeed, he had a sudden desire to get rid of his friend, to be alone with the delightful Miss Smythe and to give the ravenous gossips something scandalous to devour.

The low hum of feminine chatter alerted him to the matrons' approach. Tristan had less than a minute if he planned to make his escape through the shrubbery. The guests wandering about at the top of the garden would not suspect a solitary gentleman of any impropriety.

"What do you want to do, Miss Smythe?" Tristan said with some impatience.

Miss Smythe pursed her luscious lips and glanced down at her slippers. One could almost hear the cogs turning as she considered her options.

"Are you able to provide for me, sir?"

Matthew struggled to suppress an arrogant smirk. The lady would have no complaints. Of that he was certain. "Have no fear. I shall ensure all your needs are met."

A pink blush touched Miss Smythe's cheeks, and she inclined her head. "Then I accept."

Tristan muttered a curse, turned and threw his hands in the air.

A pleasurable thrum of anticipation raced through Matthew's veins at the prospect of bedding the beauty before him.

How odd.

The sensation soothed his bruised pride. It made him forget that, a mere thirty minutes before, he had played in the most notorious card game of the Season, and lost far more than he had intended.

"You need to leave, Tristan." A sudden urgency to claim Miss Smythe's soft lips took hold. "You need to leave now." He held Miss Smythe's gaze as he gestured to the topiary archway. "Call on me tomorrow. Go before it's too late."

Tristan crept towards the exit, hesitated every third step before disappearing into the shadows.

With no time to waste, Matthew pulled Miss Smythe into his arms. The gasp that left her lips contained a hint of excitement. Her dainty hand came to rest on his chest, her fingers fluttering over his heart. It felt oddly reassuring, though he resisted the urge to inform her that the organ was nothing but a cold, hard lump of stone.

"When people gossip about our tryst, what do you want them to say about us?" Matthew asked. She shivered as his words breezed across her cheek. Such sensitivity to his touch would bode well for their coupling. "Is this to be a ravishing? Do you wish to portray a naive woman lured into a trap by a rogue?"

Miss Smythe swallowed deeply as her gaze lingered on his mouth. "Well, I do not want people to think me foolish." She shook her head. "No," she added with a hint of determination. "Given the choice, I would like them to say it is a love match. Everyone must think we were so consumed with passion we lost our heads."

Convincing others he was in love was far beyond the realms of his capabilities. *Love* was a word foreign to him. The word made the muscles in his shoulders tight, tense. The mere thought left a bitter taste in his mouth, a foul flavour only superseded by the word *trust*.

Passion, on the other hand, came as easy as breathing air. If the lady wanted to experience pure carnal lust, he would gladly give it to her.

"That is what I hoped you would say." The lascivious nature of his thoughts was evident in his tone. "From the moment we are discovered that is how we will play this game." A frisson of excitement raced through him. He needed something to distract from the trauma of the night's events, something sweet and untainted to cleanse his mind. "You have my word, as a gentleman, I will ask for your hand. But for now, I intend to kiss you with such ardent vigour I believe we will struggle to stand."

Miss Smythe pursed her trembling lips. "You … you should know I have never kissed a gentleman."

For some obscure reason he found her comment pleasing. "Then you must forgive my abrupt approach. I am afraid there is no time for gentle tutoring. Do I have your permission to continue?"

Good Lord!

Never in his life had he asked such a question.

The lady nodded, raised her chin and closed her eyes. She looked serene, angelic, and he feared he was about to sample a little piece of heaven.

Matthew took her chin between his thumb and forefinger, lowered his head until their lips touched. The sweet scent of roses filled his nostrils, the smell pure, clean, surprisingly arousing. Her lips were warm, full and soft, but he did not have time to appreciate them further.

"The fountain must be through here." A lofty feminine voice permeated the air. "Lady Morford assured me it was a sight not to be missed."

His hands followed the shape of Miss Smythe's hips, settled on her buttocks and pulled her against the evidence of his mild arousal. A tiny gasp left her lips, giving him the opportunity to delve deeper, to explore the unfathomable depths of innocence.

Matthew expected to encounter resistance, for her fear to taint the experience. He was not expecting her tongue to brush seductively against his. Nor was he expecting her to throw her arms around his neck, to press her breasts against his chest and moan into his mouth.

God help him.

All he wanted was to lower her to the ground and pleasure her until dawn. Many times he had felt the powerful grip of desire commanding the most important part of his anatomy. Yet now, an undeniable need coursed through every part of his body.

Miss Smythe's inexperienced fingers found their way into his hair, twirling, tickling, tugging at the roots. He broke for breath, his gaze falling to the swell of creamy flesh rising to greet him. A mumbled curse of appreciation left his lips and he captured her mouth with shocking desperation.

Engrossed in plundering the mouth of his maiden, he failed to respond to the series of high-pitched feminine shrieks and wails.

"Good heavens!"

"Oh, cover my eyes, Felicity. I cannot look."

"What is the meaning of this, sir?"

Despite the matrons' comments, Matthew was not ready to let his delicate flower go. He held her close, his tongue engaged in an erotic dance that promised a wealth of pleasure.

"Put the lady down this instant, sir."

Miss Smythe attempted to pull away. The action left him frustrated, ready to turn on the bloodthirsty pack of matrons and send them to the devil.

He dragged his mouth from hers though continued to rain kisses along the line of her jaw.

"Tell me you love me," he whispered in her ear. Sensing her hesitation, he added, "This is supposed to be a love match, remember."

Miss Smythe tilted her head, granting him easier access to the elegant column of her throat. "Oh, I love you." The words breezed from her lips. "I love you so much it is killing me."

Damn, she was good.

"Promise me you'll marry me," he said, calling on his rampant desire to infuse feeling into his words. "Promise me you'll be mine."

"I cannot live without you," she muttered so sweetly he almost believed it was true. "I want to spend my life making you happy."

Matthew fought the need to capture her mouth again.

A lady cleared her throat. "Will you let go of her and address us, sir!"

"I have no choice but to acknowledge them," he whispered against Miss Smythe's ear. "Do not say a word."

He looked up at the three horrified faces, their hollow cheeks and pursed lips evidence of their disdain. It took a tremendous effort not to smirk at the ridiculous array of garish gowns. With plumes of feathers, jewels and strange bows in their hair, they appeared more like the exotic birds in Lady Holbrook's aviary.

"Forgive us." He held Miss Smythe tight against his chest. The need to protect her modesty proved to be the overriding factor. A man professing undying love did not tear his lady's garments. And they were unlikely to believe Lady Morford's accomplice had grabbed her from behind the bushes to ensure it looked like a ravaging. "The lady accepted a proposal of marriage, and we struggled to contain our excitement."

Miss Smythe hid her face against his coat. He cupped her head in a comforting gesture.

"Where would we all be if we were free to express our emotions?" one snooty matron said, her tone brimming with reproof.

"Do you not remember what it was like to be in love?"

The lady with a large ostrich feather jutting out of her coiffure chuckled. "I wouldn't know. I married for money." She paused for a moment, squinted as she stared at them. "Ah, it is Mr Chandler, is it not? Are you certain it is marriage you seek?"

Matthew smiled. "Even the most hardened rogues are capable of reform."

"And who is the unlucky lady?"

He kept a firm grip on Miss Smythe's head. They would discover her identity in due course, but he'd be damned before they saw shame swimming in her eyes.

"You will read the announcement soon enough," he said.

The comment received a mocking snigger. "We shall believe it, sir, when we see you standing at the altar in St. George's."

Anger flared. He failed to repress his contempt for their hypocritical opinions.

"Then you should all hope the lady marries me." His clipped tone conveyed a wealth of loathing. "A man suffering from a broken heart can be rather foolish and unpredictable. I know enough about the licentious habits of many gentlemen to see shame brought down on the most respectable families." He considered the identities of the ladies before him. "I am certain you would not wish me to regale tales of your husband's exploits, Lady Hadden."

The ladies' shocked gasps and sudden frantic hand gestures were evidence he had made his point.

"Then ... then we wish you luck in your endeavour, Mr Chandler," Lady Hadden said, ushering the women at her side like a hen gathering her chicks. "Remember, a good marriage requires nothing more than a good man."

"I shall bear that in mind the next time I am in the company of your husband."

Without another word, the matrons turned their backs and sauntered away from the secluded area.

Matthew waited for a moment. He ran his hand along Miss Smythe's bare shoulder. "They've gone," he whispered, pleased to witness her shiver at his touch.

She gazed up at him with a look of wonder. "You certainly put them in their place."

"The only way to beat the gossips is to play them at their own game."

She stepped away, stared at him for the longest time. "What do we do now?"

With a quick shake of the head, he dismissed all lustful thoughts. "I presume you are here with a relation." He was aware her parents were dead.

"I was to attend with my aunt, but she is suffering from a fever. I came with my friend, Miss Hamilton, and my uncle is here, though someone persuaded him to play a hand of cards and I have not seen him since."

Cards?

A strange sense of foreboding took hold.

Matthew scoured his mind to recall her uncle's name. "You

live with your mother's sister, I understand." He made it his business to keep abreast of all the gossip.

"Yes, they treat me like the daughter they—" She broke off on a sob. "Oh, they will be so disappointed. How could I have been so foolish?"

He touched her upper arm. "Once Lady Morford puts her mind to something she does not care who she hurts."

Miss Smythe shook her head and gave a weary sigh. "I am far from the catch of the Season. I know you only offered marriage to save Lord Morford. It was an honourable thing to do."

Honourable? Damn! No one had ever associated the word with his name. "As your betrothed, may I give you some advice?"

Her eyes brightened. "Of course."

"People can be cruel. They will spread vicious rumours about you." No doubt she would hear some distressing things about him, too. "Rise above it. Do not intimate your looks or character are inadequate. Tell yourself any man would be privileged to call you his wife. Believe you are a diamond in a pond full of pebbles."

Dainty fingers fluttered to her chest as her breathing quickened. A smile touched the corners of her mouth though he had no notion what she was thinking.

"Now," he continued, desperate to fill the silence. "I shall find someone to bribe so we may leave here with minimal fuss. I shall inform your uncle of our intentions though I cannot recall his name."

"Lord Callan."

Bloody hell!

Mere hours ago, Miss Smythe's future had appeared bright and full of promise. Now, he did not mind admitting she had no option but to marry a scoundrel. Now, she was to learn that the place she called home no longer belonged to her family. After such heavy losses at the card table, her aunt and uncle would surely struggle to keep themselves from the workhouse.

CHAPTER 2

*H*olding the torn bodice to her chest, Priscilla waited near the fountain for Mr Chandler to return. The gown mirrored her reputation: soiled, ruined, ripped to tatters. A mere hour ago life held a wealth of possibilities. The flash of admiration in Mr Mercer's eyes while dancing the cotillion led her to conclude the mild flirtation might blossom into something more.

But Lady Morford had played Priscilla like a worthless pawn in a game of chess.

Thank the Lord, Mr Chandler saw fit to wreak havoc with the spiteful woman's plan. Like a knight of old, the gentleman had stepped forward to offer his hand, to drag her bloodied and bruised from the battlefield and promise protection.

Not even Lady Morford could have anticipated his move.

Priscilla knew little of Mr Chandler's character, other than he owned a rather grand townhouse and was an exceptional host—or so people said. The matrons spun tales of a reckless rogue. A gentleman unfit for timid debutantes. But a man willing to sacrifice freedom to save his friend surely had honour running through his veins. Besides, Lord Morford was a kind, affable soul, not at all the sort to associate with a scoundrel.

Priscilla sighed.

There was little point trying to convince herself of Mr Chandler's suitability now.

In truth, she found his rugged charm appealing. An air of mystery radiated from his persona. The dangerous glint in his eye made her heart miss a beat.

Still, none of those things accounted for her decision to accept his proposal.

The real reason sounded foolish when she examined its merit. But something about him seemed familiar. It was as though they shared a connection in ways she could not explain. If she closed her eyes, she could picture every line, every mark or imperfection on his handsome face. When he'd kissed her, well, the essence of the man proved potent. It drew her to him in some inexplicable way.

The sound of approaching footsteps disturbed her fanciful musings.

Priscilla shrank back into the shadows and held her breath. Mr Chandler strode into the concealed garden via the topiary arch. With a straight spine and an arrogant grin, he held out the thick wool travelling cloak.

"I'm afraid it's the best I could do." His gaze dropped to the ripped bodice of her gown. "It should keep the cold out and protect your modesty."

Priscilla stared at him. It occurred to her that this man was to be her husband. Was this considerate gesture one of many? Or would he grow to regret his impetuous decision?

"Thank you." With hesitant fingers, she took the cloak and fastened the garment around her shoulders. "Did you find Miss Hamilton and my uncle? Did you tell them I was ill and had to go home?"

"No." Mr Chandler tugged at the cuffs of his coat. "What I mean is I found them, but I told them the truth."

"The truth?" Priscilla sucked in a breath, gulped at the sudden rush of cool air. "But surely—"

"I said we were in love. I explained that the depth of our feelings led to an impromptu incident and now it is imperative we wed."

I said we were in love.

The words fluttered through her mind. To hear an amorous declaration fall from a gentleman's lips was all she had ever wanted. However, she'd imagined them to convey a greater depth of emotion, an intense power capable of shaking her to her core.

"But that is not the truth, Mr Chandler," she countered, knowing the reality of her situation proved vastly different from that of her daydreams.

Mr Chandler closed the gap between them, took her chin between his thumb and forefinger. "Other than Lord Morford, only we will know the truth. As far as everyone else is concerned, we are hopelessly in love." The rich timbre of his voice stirred the hairs at her nape. "You have possessed me mind and body—or so others shall believe."

His emerald eyes twinkled in the darkness. A raw, masculine essence filled the air. There was no need to wear a cloak for protection. He radiated confidence, strength in his ability to fend off an attack.

"And you have possessed me mind and body." The lie left her lips with ease. "You have captured my heart—or so others shall believe."

He lowered his head, brushed his lips against hers in a chaste kiss so opposed to the way he had claimed her mouth earlier. "Do not be afraid," he whispered. "I promised my name and my protection, and I shall be true to my word."

Priscilla forced a smile. In such a dire situation, his offering should have been enough. Was it foolish to hope for more? Was it feasible to expect a mutual affection to develop?

"You must have owed Lord Morford a great debt. When you came here tonight, I doubt you intended to take a wife." She looked into his eyes, searching for the same hint of admiration she'd noted in Mr Mercer's gaze. A sign to instill confidence in their future. But he was as unreadable as a book written in Latin.

"No. I never envisaged myself as a husband. I fear I lack the necessary qualities in that regard." Mr Chandler gave a sigh of resignation. "Under the circumstances, you can have no expectations of love." He paused. "Let's continue this conversation in my carriage. For all my faults, it is not in my nature to deceive you. A frank discussion is due."

What did he mean he lacked the qualities of a husband? Perhaps he was speaking of trust, of loyalty. Did he intend to take a mistress? Was it not a little late to tell her that now?

A strange sense of foreboding took hold. "You certainly know how to make a lady nervous."

"One should never fear honesty. Only lies and deceit make fools of us." He placed her hand in the crook of his arm. "Now, let us leave here. During the journey home, I shall tell you what I seek from our alliance. And you may do the same."

With all romantic notions quashed, she braced herself for what was to be an enlightening conversation. "If we are to wed, I suppose we should have realistic expectations."

He appeared pleased with her reply. "As with any game, without knowledge of the rules, one cannot ever hope to win."

"Indeed." Priscilla smiled though her heart sank to the pit of her stomach. A lifetime full of love and laughter was the prize for the winners of this game. Yet she suspected his motives for playing differed from hers.

They crept through the shrubbery at the end of the garden, found a door leading into the mews where Mr Chandler's carriage was waiting.

"This is Billings." He gestured to the coachman. "The man is not one for conversation but has an innate ability to navigate crowds. Now, I'm told you live on Berkley Street."

Priscilla nodded. "Yes, at number twenty." Heavens, bile bubbled in her stomach at the thought of facing her aunt and uncle.

"Take the longer route to Berkley Street, Billings." Mr Chandler removed his watch and squinted at the face. "I estimate we'll need thirty minutes to complete our business." He looked up at her as he placed his watch in the pocket of his waistcoat. A sly smile touched the corners of his mouth. "On second thoughts, make it forty-five."

"Aye, sir."

Mr Chandler assisted her into his conveyance, closed the door and dropped into the seat opposite. Despite sharing a salacious kiss in the garden, there was something far more intimate about being alone with him in the confined space.

"Well, Mr Chandler," she began, desperate to fill the silence, desperate to distract her mind. "You wished to inform me of the list of rules."

"Rules? I think not. The word suggests an element of control, rigidity. Together, we will forge an alliance that allows us to live freely, to live as we please." He leant back and rubbed his chin as his gaze swept over her. "You can begin by calling me Matthew. Only my solicitor calls me Mr Chandler, and I find it creates a certain unease."

Matthew.

Once again, a cloak of familiarity enveloped her.

"Very well. You have permission to use my given name."

"Forgive me. But I cannot recall what it is."

"Priscilla."

He inclined his head but said nothing.

Silence ensued.

"Well, I am sure you didn't need forty-five minutes to agree to use our given names," she said.

"Not at all." He glanced at her hands clenched tightly in her lap. "It is simply that I do not wish to cause offence and so must decide how best to proceed."

Nothing could make her feel more foolish than she did already.

"Does it matter? I shall appreciate your honesty, regardless." Priscilla steeled herself, held her body firm and rigid in preparation.

"Very well." Mr Chandler brushed his hand through his ebony locks. "There is nothing I could ever do or say to repay the debt I owe to Lord Morford. I do not believe I would be the man I am today had it not been for his friendship and support."

Various questions formed in her mind although now was not the time to ask.

"Lord Morford is one of the kindest gentlemen I know," she agreed.

"Indeed. Tristan has loved the same woman for many years, but Lady Morford refuses to accept his choice. As his friend, I cannot allow his mother to manipulate events to suit her own purpose. And, after all he has done for me, it eases my conscience to know he has a chance of finding true happiness."

Priscilla's shoulders sagged. They were noble words. It was reassuring to know Mr Chandler had a conscience. "You would sacrifice your own happiness for that of a friend?"

"I am not a complete martyr to the cause. Like most men, there is a limit to my benevolence." He cleared his throat. "I am a gambler by nature. What I mean is I live in the moment. I do not wallow in the past. Nor do I plan for the future."

"So you base all decisions on current feelings?" Perhaps he did find her attractive. Perhaps he also felt the strange connection that thrummed in the air.

"I base all decisions on the current situation," he corrected. "Tonight, I played recklessly at the tables. I lost more than I care to contemplate. It proved a factor in my decision to make you an offer."

The sensation of ice-cold fingers crawling up her spine made her shiver. "You used me for your own gain?" One did not need to be a wise seer to know her dowry would ease his financial burden.

"*Used* is an ugly word. We have assisted each other in order to secure our position and reputation. Trust me. All will be well."

Things could not be any worse. No doubt his penchant for gambling was the reason the matrons called him a rogue.

"Did you play in the card game?"

"Unfortunately, I did."

"How … how much did you lose? A hundred pounds?" One could but hope. "A … a thousand?"

He swallowed audibly. "Too much."

Too much!

"What happened to your desire for honesty? Is vagueness not a mere mask for deceit, Mr Chandler? Let me at least hope I am not marrying a hypocrite."

"You're right." His raised brow conveyed a hint of admiration. "Forgive my lack of clarity. I lost ten thousand pounds this evening."

Priscilla covered her mouth with her hand for fear of blurting an obscenity. "Ten thousand," she eventually said. "Am I to understand you lack the funds to pay?"

"The full amount would pose a problem." His tone held no hint of shame. "I can raise almost half the sum."

Heaven help her. What sort of person gambled with money they didn't have?

"And do you plan to pay the debt with my dowry?"

"I do."

The reality of the situation hit her like a hard slap to the face. She jerked her head back, blinked to clear her blurred vision. Her mind scrambled amidst the chaotic thoughts hoping to find a way to extricate herself from her obligation.

"And what if I refuse to marry you?"

He shrugged. "Then I shall have no option but to seek other methods to raise the funds I need. In your case, I expect every fortune hunter in town will come knocking."

"The words *cold-hearted devil* spring to mind." What a naive fool she was!

"Is that your way of saying you've changed your mind?" he continued. "If so, let me offer a more detailed explanation that might sway your judgement somewhat."

She waved a hand for him to continue. "I may as well hear it all."

"It was not bad luck that I lost such a significant sum. Indeed, Lord Callan was just as unfortunate."

Priscilla shot forward. "My uncle? But he has no experience with gambling. He would never squander money in such a fashion." Henry Callan was honest, dependable, forever lecturing on the need for prudence. "You have made a mistake. You did say you'd forgotten my uncle's name."

Mr Chandler stared down his nose. "There is no mistake. You will discover the truth soon enough. I am convinced we were both duped by sharps."

"Sharps!" Priscilla flopped back into the seat. Fate was determined to cause total devastation. "Some speak of ruthless play at the gaming hells, but surely Lord Holbrook attracts a better clientele."

"Even peers use unscrupulous methods if it means saving their estates. Gentlemen fleeced us, not rogues. The stakes were high, and so the temptation to cheat is great."

Priscilla touched her fingers to her temple. No doubt someone had tricked her uncle into playing. The man would not willingly play deep. Heavens, he insisted on reusing the tea leaves when they had no visitors.

"How … how much did Uncle Henry lose?"

"A little more than I."

"What?" Anger surfaced. "How much more?"

"Lord Callan lost fifteen thousand, though I'm told that is not his only loss this month."

Priscilla put her hand to her head. The slight sense of disorientation had nothing to do with the excessive rocking of the carriage. "Fifteen thousand! Fifteen thousand?"

"If it is any consolation, the sharps added laudanum to our port. Not enough to make it obvious but enough to cloud our judgement."

"They drugged you?" Good Lord, yet another shocking revelation. "If you were not of sound mind when you played then I doubt you were of sound mind when you offered marriage."

"Perhaps not."

An odd puffing sound left her lips. "Well, should honesty be the foundation for a successful union, we have nothing to fear."

"Does that mean you intend to accept me?"

Only a fool would marry him under the circumstances, but she'd spent the night making one foolish decision after another. "I have no notion what to do. Lady Hadden is a frightful gossip and would have recognised me. I am doomed either way."

Without warning, he crossed the carriage to sit at her side and cupped her face between his large hands. "Then let me offer some form of recompense for your plight."

As soon as his lips touched hers, a fire sprang to life in her stomach. Mr Chandler's skilled tongue penetrated her mouth. The tantalising strokes teased the senses. It was impossible to resist him.

Heavens above!

Within seconds, her breathing grew ragged as she tried to contain a surge of raw emotion. Hot hands caressed her body. The arousing smell of bergamot flooded her nostrils. His essence consumed her. She was a slave to his will. Her skin tingled, burned to feel the heat from his body.

"You will find pleasure in the marriage bed," he drawled as they broke for breath. "I sense the spark of attraction between us and believe you will welcome my attentions with optimism."

His hypnotic pull proved potent. When he kissed her, she almost believed his proposal had nothing to do with helping Lord Morford, nothing to do with needing her money.

"What will become of us if we wed?" She hadn't meant the words to leave her lips. In truth, she suspected she would grow desperate for his taste, crave his attention like a bittersweet addiction. "What if we are both miserable and unhappy?"

"I shall provide for your every need."

Material needs perhaps but never emotional.

"Is that not what every lady wants?" he continued. "A life of comfort, a life free from worry."

Comfort had never been a priority.

"If I'm to be your wife, I assume you will have certain expectations." She imagined more kisses but struggled to picture anything else.

"A few. But there is only one thing I must insist upon."

Priscilla held her breath in anticipation.

"I do not own land," he continued. "I have an income from my late father's estate but earn my living hosting parties for the dissipated members of the *ton*. During the day you will be free to do as you please. But should I be entertaining guests, you are to remain in the bedchamber for the duration of the evening."

He would keep her hidden away like a naughty child? "But surely people will expect your wife to act as hostess."

"It is not that sort of party."

"What sort of—" Priscilla's cheeks flamed as realisation dawned. "Oh, I see. You mean married men cavort openly with their mistresses. Inhibitions are relaxed. They—"

"Indeed."

Having no desire to witness the unscrupulous events, she would gladly remain in the bedchamber. Suspicion flared. Despite having little choice but to marry, she refused to suffer humiliation.

"I agree to your request," she said, even though his hard tone suggested she had no option. "But I have one question and insist on an honest answer."

He sat back in the seat. "Then please continue, Priscilla."

To hear her name fall so languidly from his lips made her heart thump hard in her chest. If only she were immune to his charm. "Do you have a mistress?"

Mr Chandler frowned. "By mistress, do you mean a woman I court regularly and support financially?"

Priscilla bit down on her lip and nodded.

"Then, no. I do not have a mistress."

That did not answer the question. "But you are intimate with women."

"I am not a monk, Priscilla. I have not taken a vow of chastity."

"Then let me be blunt, sir. Do you intend to be faithful during our marriage?"

"Contrary to popular belief, I am a man of my word. If I make a promise, I keep it."

Why could he not say yes or no? "I need a more definitive answer."

"Then, yes. It is my intention to be faithful during our marriage."

"And do you intend to share my bed?"

"On occasion. When the need arises."

Oh, how dreadfully unromantic. "Do you expect my loyalty in return?"

"Absolutely. That is not a matter for negotiation." Mr Chandler removed his watch, checked the time and pushed the item back into his pocket. "Now, do we understand one another?"

"Perfectly." She was an optimist at heart. An ability to

converse honestly would stand them in good stead. The rest was in the hands of Fate.

Mr Chandler sat forward and shrugged out of his coat.

"The night is far too cold to sit in shirtsleeves," Priscilla said, sounding more like a mother than a prospective wife.

He threw his coat onto the seat opposite. "I doubt I'll be cold with you at my side. We have twenty minutes until we reach Berkley Street and I thought we could use the time to become better acquainted."

Priscilla straightened, unable to keep the grin from forming. No gentleman had ever asked about her hobbies. "What would you like to know?"

A sinful smile touched his lips. "It is not what I want to know, Priscilla, but more what I want to do."

"Oh." For the umpteenth time this evening her cheeks flamed.

"Don't worry." He tugged at the ribbons of her cloak, pushed the thick material from her shoulders. "I'll need a comfortable bed when I claim your body. For now, I would like to test a theory."

"What ... what theory?"

He brushed her cheek with the backs of his fingers. "That a raging passion lies beneath your prim exterior. That our wedding night will prove to be more than satisfactory."

CHAPTER 3

a dull thud echoed through the study. Lord Callan banged the mahogany desk with such force the lids of the ink pots rattled on the hinges. The man's eyes bulged. His complexion resembled a rainbow of hues: pink, red, purple with a hint of blue.

"You have the nerve of the Devil, sir!" Saliva bubbled at the corners of Lord Callan's mouth. He stabbed his fat finger at Matthew, seated on the opposite side of the desk. "I'll not agree to it. Do you hear me? I'll not sentence the girl to a life with a scoundrel."

Lord Callan was a blasted hypocrite. The man owed so much money his creditors were liable to tear the breeches from his bulbous behind to raise a shilling.

"Would you prefer to see her scrubbing floors in the workhouse?"

Lord Callan's cheeks ballooned. "Workhouse! Good God, man, it will not come to that."

"Then you possess the funds to pay your gambling debts?"

The man's mouth opened and closed numerous times. "My …

my private business is no concern of yours. Everything would have worked out perfectly had it not been for your untimely intervention. Lady Morford assured me her son would make my niece an offer of marriage."

Suspicion flared.

Had Lord Callan approved of Lady Morford's plan to force a betrothal? It certainly explained why he allowed Miss Smythe to roam the garden freely.

"I see." Matthew narrowed his gaze. "You risked your niece's reputation in the hope of settling your debts. Lord Morford is a generous man and would not allow his wife to suffer the shame of an uncle sent to debtors' prison."

The chair creaked under the pressure of the lord's squirming buttocks. "You insult me with such a remark."

"It is only an insult if it is not true. Desperation has a way of suppressing a man's morals. Those with an addiction often justify abandoning their principles."

"And you would know." Lord Callan gave a contemptuous snort. "Condemn me if it satisfies you, but I'd rather my niece wed a respectable gentleman than a reckless rogue."

Surely the lord was not naive enough to think Miss Smythe had a better option. Only a disreputable man would offer for a woman compromised in a garden.

"Reckless rogue?" Matthew scoffed. "Jibes don't offend me. I recognise there's an element of truth to your words."

The lord's face flamed. "So you admit you're a libertine?"

"*Restraint* is not a word in my vocabulary. But we digress. I am assured Lord Morford will not offer for your niece. The lady will tell you so herself. I, on the other hand—"

"I'll rot in hell before I let you ruin the girl."

Matthew put his fist to his mouth and cleared his throat. "It is a little late to worry about her virtue. I ravished Priscilla in front of witnesses."

"God damn you. How dare you speak of it so blatantly. Have you no shame?"

Shame? After his father's dishonourable conduct, shame had been his constant companion. But he was a man now not a boy. He'd let the Devil damn him before he gave the emotion merit.

"Weak men feel shame, my lord." And cowards who chose to run away from their problems.

"Dishonourable men feel indifference, Mr Chandler."

Matthew gave a weary sigh. There was only one way to bring an end to the gentleman's mindless rants.

"I fear there is not an ounce of sense in your addled brain." Matthew stood. "I bid you a good day, my lord." With a curt nod, Matthew turned and made for the door.

"Where the hell are you going?"

"You have made your position clear. Allow me to inform you that you leave your niece no option but to elope."

"Elope? Elope!" The gentleman slapped his hand to his chest. "Heavens, are you determined to send me to my grave?"

Matthew grasped the handle. "Good day."

"Wait! Wait." Lord Callan cleared his throat. "If you profess to love my niece as you say, you would not put her through the indignity of an elopement."

Matthew turned to face him. "If you love your niece as much as I suspect, you would not deny her a wedding in St George's. Other than the fact you consider me a rogue, do you have any other objection?"

Lord Callan waved to the empty seat. "Loath me to point out the obvious, but you are not the sort of man to … to settle."

Confident he'd made his point and that the lord realised he had limited options, Matthew dropped into the chair. "Nor am I the sort who falls in love. But one never knows what Fate has in store."

Lord Callan jerked his head. "You expect me to believe you love the girl."

Girl? Matthew had touched Miss Smythe's soft curves, cupped her round, full breasts. The lady was a woman in every sense of the word. Well, in all but one. And he would soon rectify that problem despite never having deflowered a virgin.

"Love is not an easy emotion to feign," Matthew said. Although when one was skilled in the art of seduction, many ladies had been known to mistake lust for love. "Call the lady down. Draw your own conclusions."

A weary sigh breezed from Lord Callan's lips. "The girl's upset with me. I assume you were the one who told her of my losses at the table."

"I refuse to lie to her. If she is to marry me, we must have complete honesty between us." Whether either of them accepted the truth was another matter entirely. "You may be interested to know I have my suspicions about the credibility of the card game."

"I knew it!" The grey-haired lord leant forward, his countenance suddenly improving. "You suspect cheating?"

Matthew nodded. "Cheating on a grand scale. Did you intend to play so deep?"

"Oh, I like to have the odd flutter, a small wager here and there."

The odd flutter? The man had more of a problem than he cared to admit.

"Forgive my directness, but fifteen thousand pounds is by no means a small wager."

"I never meant for it to go that far. I was on a winning streak and thought it a prime opportunity to repay my vowels. One minute we'd won eight tricks the next …" The gentleman dragged his hand down his wrinkled face. "Do you think they marked the cards?"

"Not that I'm aware." Matthew had observed the cards during the first few hands of whist. Cheating to that degree required skill in deception. It required a group of men working together, collaborating. "But I intend to look into the matter."

He would do a damn sight more than that.

"Then I shall make a few discreet enquiries of my own." Lord Callan narrowed his gaze. "You asked of my objection. It is your predilection for illicit pursuits that leads me to doubt your ability to commit to my niece."

Matthew had no problem with commitment. It was love and trust that chilled his blood. "I have made a promise, and I am a man of my word. I make my living catering to other people's illicit pursuits. My skill lies in that of a generous host, nothing more."

"Everyone knows all the best hosts participate in the evening's entertainment," Lord Callan countered.

Matthew chuckled to himself as it was rather a naive view. "I am not a great lover of horses, yet I own a stable full of them. Pretence is often necessary for survival."

"That is what I fear. My niece thinks with her heart, not her head. It would not take much to convince her of your affection. The girl is as foolish as her mother."

The sudden urge to defend Miss Smythe took hold. "What is foolish to you seems sensible to me. The heart never lies, my lord."

"Damn it all." Lord Callan snorted. "You must be in love with the chit if you believe that nonsense."

Under present circumstances, Matthew did not wish to correct his misconception. "Then am I to take it you agree to the match?"

"Agree? Of course not. But what choice do I have?" The man threw his hands in the air. "The girl seems smitten and will come of age in a few months. Her head is so full of romantic hogwash she's liable to flee to Gretna."

A profound sense of relief filled Matthew's chest. Miss Smythe's dowry was within his grasp. But oddly that was not the primary reason for the sudden rush of excitement coursing through his veins. He wanted the golden-haired beauty in his bed. He wanted her curvaceous form sprawled between his sheets. Damn. It had been an age since he'd lusted after a woman.

Once he'd satisfied his sinful cravings, he would need to handle the situation delicately. They could be friends, occasional lovers, but never more than that.

CHAPTER 4

*A*fter a glorious week of sunshine, their wedding day suffered a torrential downpour with puddles deeper than a copper bathtub. A loud crack of thunder echoed beyond the roof of St. George's. A sudden gust rattled the doors. The wind found a way through the gaps and crevices and rushed down the aisle to whistle its objection. Two gentlemen hurried from the box pews and pushed against the doors as though fighting to keep the Devil out.

Despite the formidable storm, the rector's monotone voice recited the relevant passage from the *Book of Common Prayer*.

Priscilla's hands shook. Perhaps it was an omen. Perhaps their lives were to be as bleak as the weather. She struggled to hold Mr Chandler's assured gaze. Needing to rouse an ounce of faith in the future, she glanced beyond the altar at the painting of the *Last Supper*.

The biblical scene brought little comfort.

"You're allowed to smile," Mr Chandler whispered whilst holding her hands. "This is a love match after all."

"Promise me all will be well." Her chin trembled though it

had nothing to do with the draughty stone building. "Promise me we're not making a mistake."

"I promise."

The pledge was oddly reassuring, totally believable. The firm grip of his hands, the playful grin illuminating his handsome face, gave her the confidence to continue. With her mind in a bit of a daze, she went through the motions, speaking when required, not really listening to the rest of the service. Once the declaration was made—the pronouncement that they were joined in the eyes of God—her fears faded.

Still, she felt lightheaded, dizzy, detached from reality. Had she not been able to hold Mr Chandler's arm while passing through the group of well-wishers hugging the door, she would have crumpled into a heap.

"Come," Mr Chandler said as they hovered under the shelter of the portico. "A little time alone in the carriage will lift your spirits. We'll circle the park to give our guests time to reach the house before we arrive." He cupped her elbow, and they raced down the steps. After fumbling with the wet handle on the carriage door, he assisted her inside.

"The rain is coming down so hard one might think the Lord wants to wash away our sins." Priscilla shook a few droplets of water from her fingers and dabbed her cheeks.

"It would need to rain for forty days and nights to rid me of mine." Mr Chandler sat back in the seat opposite, removed his hat and brushed his hand through his hair. "But you have done nothing to warrant His censure."

"Have I not just sworn to love you?"

"And you will." He squirmed in the leather seat, but she doubted the movement had anything to do with a broken spring. "If only in the physical sense."

Heavens, he would expect her to share his bed this evening. The thought brought conflicting emotions. While nerves created a hollow cavern in her stomach, the promise of more kisses heated her blood.

"Is that how you interpret the vow?" she asked. As a man who stressed the importance of honesty, she had wondered how he wrestled with his conscience.

"The ancient Greeks recognised six different varieties of love. I intend to follow the theory of Eros and worship you with my body. I lack the ability to give more than that."

It was an odd conversation to have on one's wedding day. "You believe yourself incapable of any deep and long-lasting affection?"

"The poets claim that love is the pinnacle of happiness. In my experience, love brings nothing but pain. Therefore, one must cultivate happiness in other ways."

The comment proved enlightening. To speak of such a pain, he must have loved once. The thought roused a flicker of hope. There was every chance he could learn to love again. But what was his story? Had a lady broken his heart? Had his father's death left a permanent scar?

"When you speak of cultivating happiness are you referring to your love for gambling and a crowd of dissipated debauchers?" She hadn't meant to mock.

His raised brow conveyed an air of displeasure. "I speak of my love for independence, for a mind free from worry and a heart free from shame."

Shame? It was an odd word to use.

Priscilla studied his profile as he gazed out of the window. His full and wickedly sensual lips were drawn thin. His muscular shoulders sagged. No doubt his eyes swam with sadness as he observed the rivulets of rain running down the glass pane. Somewhere inside he harboured a profound sorrow.

Priscilla's heart thumped against her ribs as the need to soothe him took hold. "So, my new home is to be on Grosvenor Street," she said, hoping a change of subject would lighten the mood.

When he turned to face her, his mask of indifference disguised any hint of sadness. "I live at number twenty-six, or should I say *we* do. The house is the only one in the row with a long garden and access to the mews. Both aspects have proved useful for entertaining on a grand scale."

"Then I must assume there are topiary hedges tall enough to conceal any activity beyond." One did not need experience in illicit liaisons to know why some couples favoured the garden. "No doubt you have a small summerhouse and auction the key to the highest bidder."

Mr Chandler's eyes widened. "That is an excellent idea. I have a wooden garden room but never thought to charge for its use."

She gave a satisfied sigh. "Perhaps a gentleman will be so desperate to spend time alone with his mistress he'll cover the cost of repaying your vowel."

"There are men foolish enough although ten thousand pounds is rather a big ask." A chuckle left his lips. When he smiled, his emerald eyes glistened like dew on a blade of grass.

Goodness, she really should rein in her romantic musings.

"You'd be surprised," she said, dragging her thoughts away from the dimple on his right cheek. "I imagine the gentlemen who attend your parties are full of their own importance. You only need to persuade one of them to offer an extortionate sum, and the rest will follow. You could decorate the space in a theme that might prove enticing."

Mr Chandler rubbed his chin. "And what would you find enticing, Priscilla? Where would a man take you if he hoped to lure you into temptation?"

The rich, languid tone to his voice sent a shiver racing from her shoulders to her toes. How was she to answer? Other than the few kisses she had shared with Mr Chandler she knew nothing of intimate relations. Even so, she imagined somewhere warm, sumptuous, comfortable.

"Aunt Elizabeth told me that Lord Banbury has a sultan room. The exotic always draws a crowd. Have you seen it?"

"No. I've heard tales of Banbury's extravagance but suspected they were overrated."

"Reams of red silk line the walls. Plush velvet cushions litter the floor. Those who enter must remove their shoes. The ladies can try on bracelets with charms, anklets that jingle. The theme lends itself to decadence. Whenever Lord Banbury opens up the room, there is always a crush."

"And you suggest I create such a place at home?"

"It would certainly prove to be an attraction."

Mr Chandler studied her. "I didn't realise I'd married a woman with a head for business."

Most men would not allow their wives to speak so freely. "If you object to my input, then please say so."

"On the contrary." He snorted. "I welcome your opinion. Never feel you cannot be open and honest."

She tilted her head. The man surprised her at every turn. "Perhaps I might be useful to you occasionally."

His gaze travelled slowly over her. "I'm sure you will." The simple statement sounded like a lascivious promise.

A vibrant energy filled the air. The mutual attraction was undeniable. With his hungry gaze and parted lips, he gave every indication he eagerly awaited the intimacy married couples shared.

"What a shame we must join our guests this morning," he continued. "A private celebration would have been a far better option."

Priscilla breathed deeply. Her husband had a way of heating her blood with a few innocent words. Then again, he was skilled in seduction.

"There is no need to keep up the pretence when we are alone, Mr Chandler."

The smile gracing his lips carried a hint of pity. "Whatever is said between us will always be the truth. You will soon learn that love and desire are separate things entirely. I do not need to feel any long-lasting affection to be intimate with you. And we are not in our dotage, Priscilla. You will call me Matthew."

Before she had a chance to reply, the carriage rattled to a stop outside number twenty-six Grosvenor Street. A footman dressed in blue and white livery assisted her descent as another rushed to greet them with an umbrella.

"Welcome to your new home." Matthew placed his hand on the small of her back and guided her into the hall. "I thought you could meet the servants briefly. Tomorrow you may confer with Mrs Jacobs, the housekeeper, and then consult me on any changes you wish to make."

Priscilla scanned the line of cheerful staff. "There are rather a lot of footmen for a house in town." She counted six. The men were all tall, broad and muscular, a little too coarse in appearance when compared to the servants in all the best houses.

"I entertain here twice a week. Sometimes the crowd can be a little hard to tame," he said as though party to her thoughts. "While I am handy with my fists, it is wise to have men to call upon when needed."

"I see." An image of drunken lords brawling on the dance floor flashed into her mind, of scantily clad ladies giggling at the raucous display.

"This is Hopkins." Matthew gestured to the butler, a man also lacking the refined air considered a prerequisite for the position. His features challenged all preconceptions: a flat, squashed nose as opposed to one long and straight with razor-sharp edges. Hopkins' face was full, his lips thick rather than the hollow cheeks and thin disapproving mouth she was used to.

Hopkins bowed. "Should anything not be to your satisfaction, madam, please bring it to my attention at once," he said with eloquence. Based on his appearance, she expected his tone to be that of a man from Whitechapel. "The guests have just arrived and await you in the drawing room."

"Thank you, Hopkins."

"Some people say the bumps and scars on a man's face speak of his pugilistic abilities," Matthew said as they moved along the line.

Priscilla glanced at him and smiled. "Then I assume Hopkins has his uses."

"Indeed." He paused while the procession of servants bowed and curtsied before returning to their duties. "You will never have cause to fear for your safety with Hopkins around."

"My safety? Are your parties always so … so wild and boisterous?" Priscilla dismissed the ice-cold chill flowing through her veins. A home should be a place of sanctuary, not a place where one locks themselves away in a bedchamber expecting an attack.

"Not always, but men often argue over a mistress. The men who come here have no conscience. The dissolute care nothing for moral restraint."

Was life to be endless rounds of bawdy parties, her home abused by drunken louts? Surely there was a better way to supplement one's income?

They stopped outside the drawing room door. "Is that why I am banished to the bedchamber when you're entertaining?"

"It is my duty to protect you, Priscilla."

The comment should have reassured her, but his tone lacked the warmth necessary to suggest he cared. "And I suppose it is my duty to please you."

He smiled. "Did you not swear to obey my every command?"

Priscilla placed her hand in the crook of his arm. "Like you, my views are different when it comes to interpreting my vows."

Due to the scandalous rumours circulating regarding their need to marry, Matthew had suggested they invite only close friends and family to the house. He refused to give the gossips an opportunity to gloat. Looking at the small gathering—numbering five in total —one would assume Priscilla and Matthew were orphans. Priscilla's guests included her aunt, uncle and Miss Hamilton. Matthew invited Lord Morford, his wife of three days, Isabella, and his uncle, Mr Herbert Chandler.

"My nephew is a constant surprise." Uncle Herbert nudged Matthew. Herbert possessed such an open and friendly countenance she couldn't help but like him instantly. "Matthew insisted he would never marry and all the time he has been hiding you away."

Priscilla touched the man affectionately on the arm. "I'm sure Matthew meant to tell you of our betrothal sooner, but things progressed rather quickly."

It was the first time her husband's given name had fallen from her lips. How strange that something so simple could create a sense of intimacy.

"Love strikes the heart when one least expects it." Uncle Herbert chuckled. He was incredibly handsome for a man of middling years. "I am relieved to find my nephew is just as susceptible. I feared he would spend a lifetime alone." He grabbed Matthew's shoulder firmly. "Your father would be proud. I assume your mother was too ill to travel but what of your siblings?"

At the mere mention of family, a dark cloud descended to dull her husband's handsome features. "Beatrice is nursing my mother and Simon is too busy with estate business to leave Yorkshire."

In truth, Matthew had not given the family a choice and had only written three days ago to inform them of his impending nuptials. In the letter, he'd mentioned his mother's ill health as a way of justifying his actions, though Priscilla suspected there was more to it than that.

"I doubt Simon will believe it." Uncle Herbert laughed. "No

doubt he will think it a prank to annoy him. Perhaps when you sire heirs, it will force your brother to marry."

Matthew smiled, but his eyes were like cold mossy pools of nothingness. "Then I can only pray he finds a bride quickly. I have no intention of ever living at Moorlands."

"You may change your mind when you have a son." Herbert raised a mischievous brow.

"I doubt it," Matthew snapped.

A look of pity flashed across his uncle's face. "This is a time of new beginnings. Things will be different now. You'll see." He patted Matthew on the arm, took Priscilla's hand and pressed a light kiss to her knuckles. "I shall leave you to mingle with your guests. Lord Morford has been hopping about like a hare in his desperation to speak to you."

Priscilla met Tristan's nervous gaze. No doubt guilt formed the basis of his anguished expression. "He seems eager for our attention."

"Tristan recently married in a private ceremony, and we've not congratulated the couple." Matthew patted his uncle on the back. "We'll come and find you shortly."

"You must come to dinner," Priscilla said, much to Uncle Herbert's surprise.

"Dinner?" A smile touched the man's lips, and he cast Matthew a dubious glance. "Are you sure it would not be an imposition? My nephew usually insists on meeting me at my club."

Matthew swallowed deeply. "I can make an exception," he said, and she could not tell if he was pleased or annoyed.

As soon as Uncle Herbert moved away, Tristan hurried over. "How are you both faring?"

The ebony-haired lady at his side touched his arm. "Stop worrying, Tristan." She turned to Priscilla. "Forgive him. He holds himself responsible for your predicament."

Priscilla understood why Tristan blamed himself. But life was too short to worry. Only a few weeks prior, poor Mr Fellows had been knocked down and killed by a carriage whilst crossing the road on a foggy morning.

"Your mother is the only person who should feel remorse," Priscilla said.

"It might please you to know she now lives with my sister in Ripon." Tristan forced a weak smile. "I give you my word she will not trouble either of you again." He turned to Matthew. "I know I have said so a thousand times, but I'll not forget what you've done for me, for Isabella, for all of us."

Matthew snorted. "As I have already explained to my wife, I am not a martyr, Tristan. At heart, I have always had selfish tendencies. Do not give the matter another thought. Besides, have you not heard the news?"

"What news?"

"We're in love." Matthew gave a sinful smirk. "Surely it's obvious."

Despite knowing it was far from the truth, butterflies fluttered in Priscilla's chest. The tickling sensation travelled to other parts of her body as her husband brought her hand to his lips and brushed a tender kiss over her knuckles. The same playful glint she'd seen when alone with him in the carriage flashed in his eyes. Lust, it seemed, could be mistaken for love if one was of a mind to deceive.

Tristan and Isabella stared at them.

"Then I would say the course of true love is rarely smooth." A dubious look marred Tristan's fine features. "Should either of you need anything while navigating the turbulent waters, you only need ask."

Isabella nodded. "Our door is open, day or night."

Matthew raised his chin. "There is no need for concern. In my tainted experience, we share the one thing most married couples lack—honesty. There are no secrets. We understand one another and so how difficult can married life be?"

CHAPTER 5

Standing together in the hall, Matthew and Priscilla were all smiles and chuckles as they said goodbye to their guests. Her aunt and uncle were the last to leave.

"Now, if you need any help with the household management you know where to come," her aunt said in earnest.

Matthew almost snorted. The Callans were the last people to offer advice on handling one's affairs.

"I'm sure I shall need your help with many things." Priscilla clutched her aunt's hands. "Once I've settled in here I shall be sure to call round."

A frisson of guilt flashed through him. Despite knowing of her family's failures, his wife showed nothing but kindness and respect to her kin.

"When you're settled we might go shopping." Aunt Elizabeth's comment surprised him. Perhaps the woman knew nothing of her husband's financial predicament.

"Shopping?" Lord Callan tutted. "Ladies and their fripperies."

A smile lit up her aunt's face. "Perhaps we might treat ourselves to new perfume from Floris."

"That would be wonderful," Priscilla replied, although he noted the lack of enthusiasm in her tone.

"Well, Chandler," Lord Callan said, tugging at his collar as though struggling for air. "We'd best be off. No doubt my solicitor will be in touch in the next few days."

No doubt? Damn right he would be. "I shall look forward to the event."

Once left alone, an uncomfortable silence ensued. Despite outward appearances, Matthew doubted the transformation from bachelor to husband would be without its problems.

What the hell did a man do with a wife, other than the obvious?

Priscilla shuffled from one foot to the other, twiddled her fingers and sighed. "Well, now would be a good time to give me a tour of the house. Hopkins arranged for the footmen to take my luggage upstairs, so it remains for you to point me toward my bedchamber. Perhaps it would ease the tension if we got the preliminaries over with."

Her nervous ramblings caused guilt to flare. Regardless of the promises made, he was unaccustomed to pleasing anyone but himself. Nevertheless, he wanted to make her happy. It seemed like a fair exchange. What sort of man would he be to take a lady's money and give nothing in return? But where the blazes was he to start?

His skill with women lay in one specific area.

"Preliminaries?" He cast a mischievous grin though doubted she meant the claiming of her body. "Are you so eager to get the deed done? If you're referring to the business of marriage, then I would rather savour the moment not rush."

The apples of her cheeks flamed. "I … I was referring to the mundane tasks of settling in."

"You'll soon come to know that I'm uncomfortable with all mundane aspects of life." He moistened his lips. "I refuse to temper my wild imagination and hope there will be nothing ordinary about settling in."

"It … it appears we are having different conversations."

"Once we begin, I'm sure we'll be singing the same tune." Damn. For a man who'd spent years avoiding marriage, he sounded desperate to consummate their union. Then again, since the night he'd promised to wed her, he'd not looked at another woman, let alone satisfied his carnal needs.

"Did you mind me inviting Herbert to dinner?" She bit down on her bottom lip. The abrupt change of subject was perhaps a way of settling her nerves. "It is obvious he admires you greatly, and it would give us an opportunity to become better acquainted."

"There has never been a need to invite him before as we meet each week at Boodle's." Herbert Chandler never sat in judgement. He never spoke of the past. In that regard, he was an ideal companion. One could only hope Priscilla did not feel the need to pry into their family history. "But perhaps we should wait until we're more at ease with one another."

"Do you find me too presumptuous?" Two thin lines appeared between her brows. "Here we are married for little over an hour, and already I am organising your diary."

"Had I any objection, I would have said so."

They stared at one another. Neither knew what the hell to do or say next. Damn it all. Marriage proved to be harder than he'd imagined.

"Come, let me show you to your bedchamber." He gestured to the stairs. "You can wash and change before dinner." And he needed time alone to decide how best to proceed.

Priscilla touched her stomach. "After such a wonderful wedding banquet I doubt I'll have room to eat again today."

"Then we must find a way to work up an appetite." The comment roused the memory of their heated kisses in the carriage. Judging by the slight tremble of her chin, she understood his meaning perfectly.

"Will we be sleeping together?" She struggled to hold his gaze.

Was it a trick question? "Excuse me?"

"Are we to share a chamber or will we have separate rooms?"

"I thought separate rooms would be best." A man needed the freedom to strut around naked. And having experienced many illicit liaisons, one woman's body looked much the same as another. It was the intimacy of seeing her wash and brush out her hair that threatened to destroy his equilibrium. "We will both want privacy."

Rather than her tight shoulders sagging with relief, she narrowed her gaze. The look suggested he had made a grave error. How odd.

"I understand." She nodded. "You do not want to make excuses to be alone. But you should know that I will not make demands on your time. I am not a woman who moans or mithers. I am not a leech intent on sucking you dry."

Bloody hell!

Did the lady not understand that certain phrases forced a man to think wicked thoughts? He considered her full pink lips, imagined threading his fingers through her hair as she knelt before him.

Eager to experience the fantasy, his cock swelled and pushed against the fall of his breeches. Matthew swallowed hard. Damn. He could not take his bride in the middle of the afternoon. It suggested an element of desperation, suggested he lacked control.

"No doubt we will have cause to reassess the living arrangements as problems arise." To tell her they might sleep together at night would only give false hope. Besides, most married couples slept separately. "Nothing is set in stone. For now, I suggest we continue as planned."

"Then lead the way," she said with an air of resignation.

Matthew gave a curt bow and motioned to the stairs. "After you."

He followed behind, observed the gentle sway of curvaceous hips, pictured the same scene minus the clothes.

Coming to a halt on the landing, she waited for his direction.

"Your bedchamber overlooks the garden." He walked to a room further along the corridor, opened the door and stepped back for her to enter. "It's generally quieter unless I'm hosting an event. Hopefully, no one will disturb you."

With some hesitation she stepped inside, twirled around to scan the decor, stroked the dusky-pink bed hangings as her wide eyes focused on the large four-poster bed.

Matthew cleared his throat. "I'd suggest ordering new soft furnishings, but until I've repaid the vowel, it is best to be prudent."

"These will be perfectly fine. Where do you sleep?"

"The master suite is next door. You can access my chamber via the connecting door in the dressing room though I took the liberty of locking it. The key is on the night table next to your bed. That way there is no fear of waking at night to find a stranger lurking in the shadows."

Priscilla arched a brow. "You're my husband, Matthew, not a stranger." She wandered over to the window. "Do the guests realise you can see behind the topiary hedge from up here?"

"When in the throes of passion, I doubt they give the matter much thought. Why? Do you intend to snoop on their amorous activities?" The notion of her experiencing pleasure at the sinful sight aroused him further.

"A lady must do what she can to further her knowledge."

The minx was teasing him. "Have no fear. I shall give you all the tutoring you need. Trust me you'll never have cause to look elsewhere."

Averting her gaze, she touched the burgundy drapes, unhooked the sash and drew the curtains.

Once plunged into semi-darkness, all thoughts turned to seduction. After all, she was his wife. Duty demanded he bed her.

Indeed, his cock ached to burst free, to push inside and experience the true depth of innocence.

"And what are your plans for the evening?" Confidence infused her tone which was surprising when one considered the intense pulse of desire radiating through the room. "Am I to come to your chamber?"

"No. I will come to you." It was easier that way. He could leave, sneak out as soon as she fell asleep. It would save any awkward conversations.

"Then you do intend to lie with me tonight?"

"Of course." He sounded far too eager. "Our alliance must be legally binding."

"I see." With deft fingers, she pulled the pins from her hair. Golden curls fell free to drape over her shoulders and slide seductively down her back.

"What are you doing?" Good Lord. For the first time in his life, his heart fluttered in his chest.

"I see little point in waiting," she said, placing the pins on the dressing table. "If it is to be an exercise simply to satisfy legalities then I would rather get it over with."

Bloody hell. He scratched his head. "Priscilla—"

"Help me out of this gown."

Matthew stood dumbstruck while Priscilla fiddled with the tiny pearl buttons.

Things were not going to plan.

To begin with, he wanted to bed his wife. Not for the pathetic reason he'd given but because he found her attractive. The lady was a constant source of amazement. At their first meeting in the Holbrooks' garden, he'd believed her to be timid, shy, easily persuaded.

How wrong could a man be?

Priscilla stepped out of her slippers and placed her foot on the stool. With delicate fingers she rolled her silk stocking down slowly over her knee, over a slim calf and trim ankle. From the sensual curve of her mouth, she must have gleaned some pleasure from the feel of the fabric gliding over her skin. Liquid fire pumped through his veins.

Heaven help him, he'd married a temptress.

"Allow me," he said, hoarsely when she raised her leg to remove the other stocking.

Priscilla caught his gaze, stopped her ministrations by way of silent permission. "Then lock the door."

Matthew did not need to be told twice.

After granting her wish, he closed the gap between them with some haste. He knelt down, placed her foot on his knee and slid his hand under her gown, up to her thigh.

The nerves in the tips of his fingers tingled as he tugged the delicate ribbon garter holding the stocking in place. The temptation to touch her more intimately took hold. With the pad of his thumb, he brushed the smooth skin above the top of her hosiery.

Priscilla gasped but did not pull away.

Matthew suppressed the grin threatening to form. Witnessing the arrogance of a seasoned seducer would only frighten her away. He captured her gaze, revelled in the sudden flash of desire he saw there when his hand edged higher.

"You're supposed to be removing my stocking," she said, the pitch of her voice strained.

Good. She wanted him.

"You cannot expect me to touch you and not give in to temptation." Nimble fingers crept higher, traced a sensual path to the intimate place between her thighs. He stroked her. Once. Twice. The third time he applied a little more pressure, continued rubbing in a slow, soothing rhythm. "Do you like that, Priscilla?"

With half-closed eyes, she whispered, "You know I do."

"Have I told you I find your honesty highly stimulating?"

"I … I am grateful you find"—she sucked in a breath—"you find my manner pleasing."

With skilled precision, his fingers continued to massage her sensitive spot. Already slick and moist, he knew she could take him. "Do you want me to continue?" he asked merely to tease a reaction.

"Continue? Oh, yes ... don't ... don't stop." Firm fingers grasped his shoulders as she struggled to keep her balance. She rocked her hips and pressed against his hand. The measured movements conveyed a hint of embarrassment, but he could feel her growing passion fighting for freedom.

As he rubbed back and forth with longer strokes, his fingers found her entrance and dipped deeper inside as he continued to build momentum.

"Do you want to feel me moving inside you, Priscilla?" Hell, his cock was as solid as a steel rod. Innocence was so bloody arousing. "Do you want everything I have to give?"

The muscles in her core hugged his fingers tight. "Yes."

One hand slipped from his shoulder. She rubbed her neck, arched her back as her body jerked in erratic spasms. Then, devil take him, his temptress let her delicate fingers drift down her neck to massage her own breast.

Bloody hell! He was about to spill himself in his breeches.

The need to thrust home almost overwhelmed him. Forcing himself to focus, he continued to pluck her strings until the sweetest moan he'd ever heard burst from her lips. Her body shook, pulsed against his damp fingers.

"There's no time to undress." The urgency in his voice was undeniable. He stood abruptly, scooped his wife into his arms and carried her to the bed. "Forgive me if this is over in a matter of minutes."

She did not reply but just stared at him with a look of glazed desire as he undid the fall of his breeches. Even when his throbbing erection sprang free, she simply lay there, the rapid rise and fall of her chest alerting him to the mounds of creamy flesh encased in silk.

The urge to see her naked took hold, to feast upon the glorious sight as he pumped hard. But to experience a deeper sense of intimacy at this stage would be a mistake.

Standing at the foot of the four-poster bed, he hooked his arms under her knees and pulled her closer to the edge. Never had he experienced the fire of anticipation flowing through his veins.

"Are you certain you want to continue?" he panted, easing her garments up to her waist. If she said no, it would be the most painful disappointment of his life.

A playful smile touched the corners of her mouth. "There is nothing I want more." Her seductive tone soothed his senses.

Heaven help him. His wife was irresistible.

With a slight tremble in his fingers as he took his cock in hand, he nudged at her entrance. When he pushed deeper, she accepted the intrusion gladly, and he could not fail to notice the look of admiration swimming in her bright blue eyes.

With her tight muscles clamped around his cock, he moved. The first few measured thrusts stoked the fire of lust burning in his veins. God, being inside his wife was so deliciously sweet he almost forgot she was a virgin.

"I can't promise it won't hurt when I push through your maidenhead," he said, "but I can promise the discomfort won't last long."

Priscilla clutched the coverlet in her fists. "Do it now then."

"I'll take it slow." He leant down, devoured her mouth as though he'd not eaten for months. He could taste berries, a hint of sweet sherry, the intoxicating essence that made every kiss they'd shared so memorable.

"You know that won't be possible," she said as they broke for breath.

Matthew angled his hips and rubbed against her as he delved deeper. He held back until she writhed beneath him—until it became difficult for her to catch her breath.

With one long hard thrust, he drove past her innocence. Sank deep.

A sudden gasp left her lips. There were no tears, no cries of anguish, nothing but a look of wonder gracing her flushed face.

He stilled, grasped her hips and held her there. The intention was to give her a moment to grow accustomed to the feel of him buried inside. But he was the one shaken.

Their gazes locked.

"I think that means I am legally your wife."

"You belong to me now." The comment was supposed to be amusing. But a strange emotion surfaced, gripped him by the throat and refused to let go. The sensation was stifling, suffocating, too difficult to define.

Damn it all. He needed to breathe. He needed to focus on the task.

She's just another woman. Forget she's your wife.

Matthew swallowed. Even in this hurried claiming, he had given too much of himself. It did not bode well for the future.

Pushing aside the chaotic thoughts filling his head, he concentrated on mastering the perfect stroke. This was simply a case of fulfilling a moment of lustful desire. He moved slowly at first, but each slide into the realms of heaven only sought to chip away at the iron casing surrounding his heart. And so he pumped in short, fast thrusts. With her sweet moans, full sensual lips, her damn arms spread out in wanton abandon, Priscilla was determined to capture him and keep him as her slave.

"Let me show you another position," he said abruptly. "Flip over onto your stomach and then come up onto your knees." This way it was easier to close his eyes, easier to ignore all the things that made her utterly beguiling.

She did as he asked without question.

With some irritation, he pushed her garments back up to her waist, ignored the deliciously round buttocks he wanted to kiss and nip. He entered her in one long deep motion, leant over and rubbed her sweet spot again until she cried, shuddered and called out his name. Then he closed his eyes and pounded hard. The

47

loud slapping of skin against skin was highly arousing and brought matters to a quick conclusion.

In all of his conquests, he'd never spilt his seed inside a woman. And he had no intention of doing so now. At the point of release, he withdrew from his wife's warm body and finished the job with his hand.

As the sound of ragged breathing filled the room, two things became abundantly clear. The depth of satisfaction he'd experienced with this woman was unique. And if he didn't bolster his defences, his life would be naught but torture and pain.

CHAPTER 6

*P*arties were always rowdy affairs.

Priscilla lay in bed staring up at the small chandelier. The glass pendants shook from the constant thrum of activity in the ballroom below. The incessant hum of the orchestra as it swept through a range of lively pieces proved distracting.

How on earth was she supposed to sleep with the continual racket?

But the commotion downstairs was not what disturbed her most. The image of her husband playing flirtatious host to a group of scantily clad women continually plagued her thoughts. Was he laughing at their salacious banter? Did they fawn over him, caress his arm in the hope they could massage another part of his anatomy? Did they twirl their fingers in his ebony hair and whisper endearments?

Would he be strong enough to fight temptation?

For the last three nights, Priscilla had waited for Matthew to come to her room. But after consummating their marriage, he'd not visited her again. On the second night, he'd opened the adjoining door in the dressing room. He'd paced back and forth for what seemed like an hour before his steps receded and the door slammed shut.

She understood his dilemma.

From her perspective, their wedding night—or afternoon to be more precise—had been spectacular. She'd given everything of herself, surrendered to the beauty of the moment. The intimate act connected them in a way she'd not believed possible. It astounded her how anyone could share their body and not feel a deep stirring of emotion.

It was all rather baffling.

When she'd joined him for dinner, he was his usual amusing self. They laughed. He tried to explain the rules of whist. When she'd leant forward to feed him her last spoonful of raspberry cake, she recognised desire in his heated gaze. And yet not once had he attempted to touch her intimately.

In one way, his reluctance to join her in bed gave her hope. Had the experience satisfied nothing but a physical hunger, he would have taken her again. He would have indulged his carnal cravings safe in the knowledge his heart was still a solid lump of stone.

So what was she to do? How was she—

A feminine shriek pierced the air.

Priscilla shot up. She clutched the coverlet to her chest, her frantic gaze locked on the door. Another loud squeal drew her attention to the window. A gentleman's gruff command to stop and wait accompanied high-pitched wails of laughter. Shuffling out of bed, she crept to the window and peered through the gap in the drapes.

Numerous couples strolled around the perimeter of the garden, the paths lit by braziers and lanterns hanging from metal crooks. At first glance, the scene was what one would expect from a society ball. But it soon became apparent that the couples were simply looking for a secluded spot to indulge their whims.

Movement near the topiary hedge to her left caught her attention. The lady's shrill cries were no more. Her gentleman had finally caught up with her but looked far from cross. With his breeches wrapped around his ankles and his bare behind jerking back and forth, he performed his wild mating ritual. The cries were now grunts of pleasure although the man's frustration radiated for a different reason entirely.

Physical release was all they craved. After her experience with Matthew, she could understand how one would yearn for the heavenly feeling. But when the sensation had subsided, what then? The level of satisfaction could not sustain a person for long.

Love, on the other hand, had the potential to last a lifetime.

Pushing away from the window, she climbed back into bed. After another thirty minutes spent tossing and turning, relief came when she heard a commotion in the hall. The front door opened and closed numerous times. The slurred farewells of the revellers were so loud it was as though they were standing outside her door.

Curious as to the identity of the men courting their mistresses, Priscilla prised the bedchamber door from the jamb and crept out onto the landing. Hidden in the shadows, she peered over the balustrade and watched the guests leave. Gentlemen ambled out into the night, some with more than one lady—though Priscilla used the term loosely—clutching their arms. A few couples lingered in the hall, their reluctance to abandon the party and return to a life of respectability causing distress.

Priscilla heard Matthew's confident voice barking orders to his footmen before he appeared in the hallway, supporting the weight of a drunken scoundrel who struggled to place one foot in front of the other.

"Help Lord Frostram to his carriage, Hopkins. Inform his coachman that he's likely to empty the contents of his stomach on the journey home."

"Shall I send a footman with him, sir?"

"No. From now on all the staff are to remain here."

Hopkins hurried forward, unhooked the lord's arm from around Matthew's neck and draped it across his own chunky shoulders. "Come with me, my lord. You'll be home and in your bed in no time." With no hint of his eloquent accent, Hopkins truly did sound like a man from Whitechapel.

Matthew brushed his hand through his hair and straightened the sleeves of his coat. "There are a few stragglers out in the garden, but that's most of them rounded up."

"As soon as I've settled his lordship here, I'll arrange for a thorough search of the premises."

"You're certain no one went upstairs."

Upstairs? Priscilla put her hand to her throat. Was that why Matthew insisted she lock the door?

Hopkins nodded. "John stood guard for most of the evening. A few tried to push past to use the bedchamber but were quickly informed of the new rules."

"Then I'd best employ another footman. We can't expect John to hold them off on his own. There's always one sneaky blighter intent on causing mischief. When in their cups, these lords will do anything to get their way." Matthew sighed. "Mrs Chandler suggested I convert the summerhouse into a room I could hire for the evening. Under the circumstances the idea has merit."

So, her husband had listened to her advice. Pride swelled in her chest.

Hopkins inclined his head, but a snigger burst from his lips. "It would solve the problem."

"Is there something you find amusing, Hopkins?"

"Not at all, sir."

"You're free to speak your mind. I'd not be able to run this debacle without your help and input."

"It's just few wives would allow such a carry-on in their home, let alone suggest ways to improve the guests' experience. Mrs Chandler is a true original, sir."

"Indeed."

The drunken lord burped, heaved and hung his head. Hopkins hoisted the man to his feet. "Well, I'd best get the lord here into the carriage before he soils the floor."

Matthew watched Hopkins drag the inebriated sot through the open doorway. From her husband's rigid stance and weary sighs, it was evident something troubled him. In her presence, he appeared so confident, so self-assured, as though there was not a problem in the world he couldn't handle.

She'd assumed he enjoyed hosting his parties. Did they not provide a constant source of amusement? Perhaps having a wife complicated matters. Separating the two different parts of his life probably proved challenging.

Well, the evening had certainly given her much to contemplate.

Priscilla was about to return to her room when a lady approached her husband from behind. The woman placed her ungloved hand on his shoulder, flexed her fingers in such a way as to suggest familiarity.

"You seem rather agitated this evening," the vixen said. "Is there anything I can do to help?"

Jealousy exploded in Priscilla's chest like a firework at Vauxhall. She swallowed down the hard lump in her throat, tried to ignore the thumping of her heart as it echoed in her ears.

Matthew turned to face the fiery-haired woman. "It has been a long night."

Her hand came to rest on his chest. "You need to relax. You need to let someone soothe away your woes."

"By someone, I assume you're offering your services." Matthew stepped back, and the woman's hand fell to her side.

Priscilla pursed her lips. The muscles in her windpipe continued to contract until she could hardly breathe.

"We've enjoyed each other in the past," the leech said, trailing her fingers across the exposed curve of her breast, "and it seems

53

we find ourselves alone this evening. I know just the thing to occupy your mind and body."

A host of unladylike curses threatened to fall from Priscilla's lips. She had a good mind to race downstairs and shove the harlot out of the door. But she would only court ridicule dressed in her prim cotton nightgown with buttons fastened up to her throat. The wife of a gentleman known for scandalous behaviour would have poise, an exotic elegance that made others gape in awe. She certainly wouldn't behave like an envious harpy and dress like a vestal virgin.

"It may have conveniently slipped your mind, Lucinda," Matthew said calmly, "but my wife is waiting for me upstairs." Did his tone carry a hint of disdain for this woman or was it wishful thinking?

The husband stealer chuckled. "The gossips say you married a mouse, not a tiger. She's not likely to make a scene if you're away from home for a few hours. Besides, she can't be a complete fool. She must know what she's let herself in for."

"You misunderstand me. Or more to the point you misunderstand the importance I place upon my vows."

"So that's why you look so terribly miserable." Lucinda gave a contemptuous snort. "I never took you for the faithful type."

"That's because you don't know the first thing about me."

"Know you? I've committed every part of your body to memory. I know what pleases you, the sounds you make upon your release. I know a virgin bride wouldn't have the first idea how to satisfy your needs."

"Your comment only serves to prove my point."

Priscilla put her hand to her heart. What was he saying? Had he found satisfaction in the marriage bed?

Lucinda raised her chin. "She must surely have the skills of a courtesan if she can keep you from straying. Well, I cannot wait to meet the virtuous creature."

"I doubt my wife would enjoy the company of dissolute rogues."

"Why not? She married you." Lucinda shrugged. "I can be patient. It's only a matter of time before you tire of her and are on the hunt for something more substantial to appease your appetite."

Matthew folded his arms across his chest. "Have you not heard? Did the gossips not tell you? We married for love, not out of necessity."

"Love?" the woman scoffed. "I am sure you are deeply in love —with her dowry."

Hopkins' heavy footsteps captured their attention.

"Have John find Miss Pearce a hackney," Matthew instructed. "It seems she's leaving alone this evening and I'll not have her walking the streets."

"It has already been arranged, sir. There are two cabs waiting outside. If you'd care to follow me, Miss Pearce."

Lucinda inclined her head. "I shall take your courteousness as a sign of hope, Matthew. Indeed, we can continue our conversation at your next gathering." She strode towards the door but stopped and glanced back over her shoulder. "I do so love a challenge. Don't you?"

Hopkins escorted Miss Pearce to her vehicle and returned almost immediately. "There was no need for a hackney. Mr Davis and his companion offered to take Miss Pearce home."

Matthew sighed. "Wait here and watch the stairs. I'll take John and Robert and scour the garden."

"Billings is waiting outside. He said you have an appointment this evening."

"God, is it that time already?"

Priscilla suppressed a gasp. Was he going out? But it was one o'clock in the morning.

With a quick glance at the long-case clock, Matthew said, "Tell him I'll be along shortly. I'll not leave here until I know Mrs Chandler is safe. Perhaps it would be wise to let a footman stand watch until I return. Whomever you choose can forgo all duties tomorrow. I won't expect to see him serving at breakfast."

"Of course, sir. I shall make the necessary arrangements."

Matthew strode off in the direction of the ballroom while Hopkins hovered near the stairs. Priscilla crept back to her chamber unnoticed. Once inside, she peered out of the window.

With an air of determination and purpose, Matthew sent the accompanying footmen off to various corners of the garden, and they scampered away like sheepdogs eager to round up the wayward flock.

While scouring the space beyond the topiary hedge looking for the bare-bottomed gentleman, Priscilla failed to notice the moment her husband glanced up at the window. When they finally locked gazes, his pursed lips and haunted expression conveyed only one emotion—guilt.

For some reason unbeknown, she placed her palm flat on the glass. It was foolish to think the gesture would bring either of them comfort. He held his hand up to her, not to wave but more a sign of recognition. Then he turned away and marched off in search of his servants.

Matthew Chandler was an enigma. One minute he was caring, passionate, a man capable of love, or so she believed. Then, in contradiction to what she knew of his character, he was often cold, indifferent, insular.

She flopped down onto the bed as she considered her dilemma. Something had to be done. If they continued in the same vein—nights spent alone, living separate lives—love would forever elude them.

CHAPTER 7

The empty seat at the opposite end of the dining table drew Priscilla's attention. Despite struggling with other aspects of married life, she enjoyed spending the first hour of the day with Matthew.

Perhaps it was a good thing he'd chosen to remain in bed. The dark circles under her eyes from lack of sleep were hardly attractive. And her mind was too preoccupied to partake in conversation. Besides, did it matter if she ate alone? Did it matter if she slept alone? She'd been doing both activities unaided for the best part of twenty years and needed no encouragement or advice.

The clock on the mantel chimed ten.

Scoundrels never rose before noon. Or so she'd heard. By the time Matthew had returned home from his mysterious appointment the birds were busy chirping their morning song.

The burning question was where in heaven's name had he been?

Priscilla drew in a breath. After his promise to be faithful, she had to trust his outing had nothing to do with bedding Lucinda Pearce. Then again, perhaps their definition of faithfulness differed. It seemed they had conflicting opinions on other matters, too. When he'd agreed to come to her bed on occasion, she'd simply not realised how infrequent that would be.

After taking numerous sips of her tea, counting the flowers on the china plate and drumming her fingers to a military tune on the table, she decided to take action.

"Right." Jumping to her feet, she stared at the portrait of a lady with windswept hair and a sultry grin. "The best things in life are worth fighting for. And every battle needs a plan."

A light rap on the door disturbed her mutterings, and Hopkins entered.

"Did you call, madam? Is everything to your satisfaction?"

Priscilla couldn't help but be amused by his lofty tone. Just like her husband, Hopkins behaved differently during the day. "I was thinking aloud. But now you're here will you inform Billings that I wish to go out?"

"Out, madam?" Hopkins cleared his throat. The lines between his brows grew decidedly deeper. "Mr Chandler did not mention an outing."

Could she not make a decision on her own? Must she have her husband's permission to breathe? Perhaps he considered it just as unsafe outside the house.

"I am to go out alone. Mr Chandler is still in his bed, and after such a late night I do not wish to disturb him."

Hopkins inclined his head. "May I be so bold as to ask if you'll be shopping? Mr Chandler will want me to advise him of your whereabouts when he rises."

"I'm to take tea with …" She could hardly visit her aunt and uncle. Neither were qualified to offer advice to a lady whose husband refused to share her bed. "I'm to take tea with Lord and Lady Morford."

Well, they had insisted she call round should she need anything. And by all accounts, Isabella's relationship with Tristan had been fraught with problems. The lady was friendly, approachable, the ideal person to act as confidante.

Priscilla glanced at the clock. It was far too early to make a social call. But she could not risk Matthew waking as he would insist on accompanying her to visit Tristan.

"Tell Billings to be ready outside in thirty minutes," she instructed firmly. It would not do to have the servants think she lacked authority. "I shall be with Lady Morford for an hour or two should Mr Chandler have any concerns."

Hopkins appeared placated. "I'll summon Billings at once, madam."

They parted company at the bottom of the stairs. She waited until Hopkins was out of sight before rushing to her room to wash her hands and put on her bonnet and pelisse. It would not be a surprise to find that the loyal servant had woken Matthew to inform him of her plans, which was why she hurried back downstairs to wait in the hall.

When Priscilla arrived at the Morfords' townhouse in Bedford Square, Ebsworth welcomed her into the hall with his usual air of indifference. Tristan's mother had invited her to tea numerous times during the last few months, her determination for Priscilla and Tristan to wed being the motivating factor.

The thought of seeing the meddling matron again sent a shiver running from her throat to her navel. Thank the Lord the woman had been shipped off to Ripon. Matthew was right about one thing: falling prey to her lies and deceit made Priscilla feel like a fool. And yet, given the option, she wouldn't change a thing.

"If you would care to wait in the drawing room, madam, Lady Morford will be with you momentarily. She insisted you make yourself comfortable."

Priscilla inclined her head. "Thank you, Ebsworth." She handed the butler her pelisse, gloves and bonnet and followed his measured steps to the drawing room. The servant walked with the grace of a duke, but she doubted he was as handy with his fists as Hopkins.

Priscilla glanced around the richly furnished room. A

pianoforte stood proudly in the corner next to a golden harp. A fine collection of sporting paintings graced the walls. An impressive crystal glass chandelier acted as a focal point, the large gilt mirror on one wall capturing the reflection.

Had Matthew not offered his hand this could have been her home. She could have been Lady Morford. An image of her husband flashed into her mind. Matthew Chandler oozed a raw masculine energy that heated her blood. His wicked hands scorched her skin whereas the thought of kissing Tristan was akin to being wrapped in a frozen blanket.

"Mrs Chandler." Isabella rushed forward and took hold of Priscilla's hands. "What a pleasant surprise. You should have sent word, and I would have been better prepared to receive you." Isabella released Priscilla's hands, brushed the creases from her dress and tucked a few stray tendrils of hair behind her ear. "I must look an awful fright."

In all honesty, Isabella looked as though she'd been tumbled in a barn. Indeed, the lady's flushed cheeks and swollen lips added weight to the theory that Priscilla had interrupted a private moment.

"Not at all, you always look splendid." Embarrassment made it impossible for Priscilla to maintain eye contact. "If it is inconvenient, I can call another time."

"No. No." Isabella waved her hands. "Please sit, and I shall send for tea."

"I do not want to impose."

Isabella pursed her lips. "It must be important else you would not have come." Pity flashed in her dark brown eyes. "And I would dearly like to become better acquainted."

Days of suppressed emotion burst forth in a long weary sigh. "I … I need to talk to someone else I shall go out of my mind."

Unperturbed by the hint of desperation in Priscilla's voice, Isabella tapped her affectionately on the arm. "Then you have come to the right place. Tell me your troubles, and I shall do my utmost to help." Perhaps it was the sight of Priscilla's trembling lips that caused Isabella to add, "On second thoughts, let us forgo the tea and have a drop of Madeira. I know it's early but … well … who's to know?"

Priscilla flopped down onto the red damask sofa whilst Isabella hurried to the side table and returned with two glasses of Madeira.

"To the goddess, Venus." With an amused grin, Isabella raised her glass in salute. "Let her wisdom guide us through the challenges we face when attempting to control our husbands."

A snigger burst from Priscilla's lips. "Is my dilemma so obvious?"

Isabella sat in the chair opposite. "You married Matthew Chandler. I did not expect things to run smoothly."

Priscilla raised her glass. "To Venus. May she give me the courage to succeed in my endeavours." She took a sip of Madeira but swallowed more than she intended. The amber liquid warmed her throat. "Heavens. Why does it taste more potent during the day?"

Isabella laughed. "I think it has something to do with having an empty stomach. But I agree, it seems stronger than usual."

There was a moment of silence.

"I suppose you're wondering why I came." Priscilla held the crystal glass in her lap, cradled between her palms. "After all, I have only been married for a matter of days."

"Forgive me for saying so, but you knew little of your husband before you married. I am not surprised you're finding it hard to settle. It will take time to grow accustomed to one another. Until then, you must bear it as best as you can."

The point was she didn't want marriage to be bearable. She didn't want to live with a stranger and pass pleasantries. As ridiculous as it seemed, she wanted Matthew to enjoy her company. Perhaps fall in love.

"I understand. I don't know why but I hoped things would be

different." After their passionate encounter on their wedding day, Priscilla had been optimistic about the future. "It's foolish of me, naive even, to expect more than he can give."

"You judge yourself too harshly. We have all found ourselves in regrettable situations. But our choices do not define us. We must learn to make the best of a bad situation. The fact you're sitting here, seeking advice, shows a certain amount of maturity and insight." Isabella offered a reassuring smile. "I'm sure you have nothing to worry about. Mr Chandler is obviously attracted to you else I doubt he would have offered marriage."

The muscles in Priscilla's throat grew tight. "What I tell you now, I tell you in confidence." When Isabella acknowledged the comment with a nod, Priscilla blurted, "Matthew married me for my dowry and because he owes Lord Morford a debt of gratitude, though I have no notion why. I'm certain my physical appearance had no bearing on his decision."

Isabella put her hand to her mouth, her wide eyes revealing her surprise. "You're mistaken."

Priscilla shook her head. "The one thing we have in our favour is we're open and honest with one another. Matthew told me he needs my money to settle a gambling debt."

"No, I mean you're mistaken about his failure to find you attractive. I saw the way he looked at you on your wedding day. I think he admires you a great deal."

"My husband admires most women." Well, that was not entirely true. He had declined Lucinda Pearce's invitation. "He has already grown tired of me."

What had she done wrong?

Isabella sat forward. "Then you have been … intimate."

A blush warmed Priscilla's cheeks. "Matthew insisted it was necessary, from a legal perspective."

"He actually said those words? How odd. The wedding night should be about more than getting one's affairs in order."

"Well, our relationship differs from most. After all, we

married out of necessity, spent our wedding night in separate rooms." Noting Isabella's blank expression, Priscilla added, "We … we consummated our … our alliance in the afternoon, once the guests had departed."

Isabella jerked her head back. "You make it sound like a business transaction."

"It was nothing like that at all." The moment would be forever ingrained in her memory. Never had she felt so complete, so happy. "It wasn't planned. One minute we were talking about our living arrangements, the next … well … I'm not sure how things progressed as they did."

With an excited gasp, Isabella clapped her hands. "Such impulsiveness only occurs when one harbours an intense passion. Your husband wants you, Priscilla, regardless of how he tries to pretend otherwise."

While his touch caused a fiery heat to course through her veins, she doubted a man with her husband's experience felt the same. "Matthew is a skilled seducer. He knows how to make lust appear as something more meaningful. If what you say is true why has he not touched me since? Two nights ago, he paced the floor outside my room for half an hour but failed to knock on the door." It was time to acknowledge the truth. "Perhaps I proved to be a disappointment. Perhaps he finds my innocence unsatisfying and prefers someone more accomplished in the bedchamber."

Isabella shot off the chair and came to sit at Priscilla's side. "But what if he feels the opposite? What if he's scared by the depth of his affection?" She patted Priscilla's hand. "What do you want from your marriage?"

A dull ache filled her chest. She wanted more than would ever be possible. "I want to learn to love him. I want him to love me in return."

A confident smile touched Isabella's lips. "Love is within your grasp. Do not underestimate your power as a woman. There are but three simple steps to make a gentleman fall in love with you."

The comment forced Priscilla to focus. "Three steps?" Oh, if only it were so easy.

"Would you like me to tell you what they are?"

"Of course." The desperation in her voice was unmistakable.

"Well, the first is lust. Matthew must feel the physical tug in his gut whenever he sees you. Bedding you must become his priority. You must seduce him without making it appear obvious."

"But I wouldn't know where to start."

"Think of it as a game. Have faith. The second is attraction. He must find you as fascinating out of the bedchamber. You must be the first thing he thinks of in the morning, the object of his dreams at night. The third is attachment. Matthew's emotional connection to you must be strong enough to suppress all fears and doubts."

Isabella made it all sound so simple, but the tasks were monumental.

"While I am desperate to make my marriage work, I cannot pretend to be someone I am not. Many of the women who attend his scandalous parties are eager to bed him. Only last night I witnessed one such lady offering her services. While I might appear desperate, I refuse to degrade myself in such a manner."

Isabella narrowed her gaze. "I hope you put the harlot in her place."

"They had no idea I was listening." She squirmed in her seat. "Matthew insists I remain in my bedchamber when there are guests in the house." The comment made her husband sound ruthless, possessive, controlling. "He says the gentlemen are unpredictable, might assume I am keen to play their games, that I will be out of my depth."

"Then he underestimates you. I attended one of his parties. I followed Tristan there as I desperately needed his advice. Yes, the guests lack morals. You'll find their behaviour shocking. But you're Mrs Chandler—the wife of one of the most desirable gentlemen in society. You're the wife of a man who fought for his place, or so Tristan tells me, a man strong enough to succeed despite courting scandal. And your place is at his side."

Isabella's encouraging words reminded her of something Matthew had said in Lady Holbrook's garden.

Do not intimate your looks or character are inadequate. Tell yourself any man would be privileged to call you his wife. Believe you are a diamond in a pond full of pebbles.

Priscilla glanced down at her plain muslin dress. "But I'll court ridicule if I stroll into the ballroom wearing a simple ivory gown. People will remember me as the plain, ordinary wife of a notorious rogue."

"No, they won't." Isabella's tone held a hint of mischief. "You'll wear something breathtaking, something elegant yet daring. Every woman in the room will wish they were you."

While the fantasy sounded wonderful, disappointment flared. "I couldn't possibly spend money on a new dress." They were yet to agree on an allowance and with the vowel still unpaid she could not be frivolous. "And everything in my wardrobe is rather dull and uninspiring."

Lost in thoughtful contemplation, Isabella stared at the floor. Then she suddenly straightened, her eyes bright with excitement. "Stand up a moment. Let me look at you." She took Priscilla's hands and pulled her to her feet. "I'd say you're an inch shorter and far more slender around the waist. We'd need to find a dressmaker willing to make alterations at short notice."

"I'm skilled with a needle and thread," Priscilla said, though was somewhat confused as to what she would be doing. "And my maid is an exceptional dressmaker. I have but two days before Matthew hosts another party."

"Two days is plenty. Wait here. I'll be back in a moment."

Less than five minutes passed before Isabella raced back into the room, her arms laden with vibrant yards of flowing fabric.

Priscilla rushed forward to help. "Have you brought your

entire wardrobe?" She removed the luxurious red dress from the top of the pile and laid it on the sofa.

"Not all, just the garments suitable for your needs." Isabella lined a sapphire blue gown, and another in black, in a row next to the red dress. "You're welcome to have all of these."

Priscilla jerked her head in shock. "But I can't take your dresses."

"I don't need them. If everything goes to plan, soon my clothes will be too tight. They'll only gather dust if left here, and it seems such a shame. Oh, and I have silk slippers to match."

Instantly drawn to the red dress, excitement bubbled in Priscilla's belly as she stroked the sumptuous velvet. "It's so generous of you, Isabella. How will I ever repay your kindness?"

"It is I who am indebted. Had it not been for your sacrifice I would not have married the man I love." Isabella offered a warm smile. "I will do anything to help you find happiness."

Struggling to contain a well of emotion, Priscilla put her hand to her chest. "Do you think I'm strong enough to enter the world of the dissolute?"

"You're stronger than you know." Isabella touched her affectionately on the arm. "Now, let's see if we can create something magnificent out of these."

CHAPTER 8

"*A*nd so I told her to keep the blasted wig on for fear of what I'd find lurking underneath. I soon came to realise her timid smile was a way to hide the fact she had no teeth."

Lord Parson snorted. "Good God, Mullworth, I know you're tight with the purse strings but what do you expect when you visit a brothel so close to the docks?"

"I think I'd prefer the feel of gums to a mouthful of rotten teeth," Chigwell said.

Matthew stood amidst the group of revellers and feigned amusement at their bawdy tales. In truth, he was tired and longed for his bed. Not knowing how to deal with his wife proved to be mentally draining.

"There's a lot to be said for those who service sailors." Mullworth chuckled. "Where else would a woman ask if you want to take a dip in the ocean of delights?"

"A dip? Surely you mean a dunking."

Raucous laughter filled the air.

"I once saw an advertisement for a woman offering her services in Whitechapel." Chigwell flapped his hand to get their attention. "As well as an extensive list of attributes she bragged of having a good leg. Leg? Leg! I thought. What about balance?"

Matthew cleared his throat. "It has nothing to do with only having one limb. The woman was referring to her stamina."

"Stamina!" Chigwell snorted. "Well, why the hell didn't she say so?"

"That's why I prefer to keep a wife in watercolour," Lord Parson offered.

"A wife in watercolour? Is it the drink that makes you spout gibberish?"

"Parson means he prefers to keep a mistress," Matthew informed suppressing a weary sigh. Was he the only one sober? "In that the relationship is easily dissolved."

The gentlemen chuckled.

"Well, we'd better hope Chandler here soon tires of his wife," Mullworth said.

The mere mention of Priscilla caused Matthew's heart to pound too quickly in his chest. To lie in bed each night knowing her warm body was just a few feet away proved torturous.

"And why is that?" Parson asked.

Mullworth tutted. "How long do you think it will be before his wife puts an end to these flamboyant parties?"

A look of horror marred the gentlemen's faces.

"Then we must find him a mistress," Parson added. "Lucinda Pearce is an exceptional companion and has not taken her eyes off him all evening. He only has to move, and she locks on to him like a hawk."

An uncomfortable knot formed in Matthew's gut. He wanted to crack a whip and throw them all out onto the street. And yet, their crude ways had never bothered him before.

"I should warn you there is not a woman here who is as fascinating as my wife." It was not a lie. There was something about Priscilla that had captured more than his interest.

"Is that why you hide the lady away?" Chigwell joked.

There were numerous reasons why Priscilla kept to her room. What sort of husband would subject her to a crowd of filthy lechers? Embarrassment played a part, too. For some unknown reason, he wanted her respect, not her disdain.

"I may share my house, but I'll not share my wife."

"Then I hope Mrs Chandler understands what it is to wed a rogue," Parson said, his attention drifting to a point beyond Matthew's shoulder. "When Lucinda sets her sights on a man, there's no getting away. The woman's claws are sharper—" He stopped abruptly, made an odd puffing sound as though he'd popped a hot piece of pie into his mouth.

"Good Lord." Chigwell's eyes bulged. "What have we here?"

Mullworth moistened his lips. "The night has suddenly become much more interesting."

Matthew swung around, eager to see what commanded their attention.

The lady in red stood confidently on the steps leading to the ballroom. It took a moment for his eyes to communicate with his brain, to acknowledge the identity of the delightful package of contradictions.

While Priscilla's angelic face radiated purity and innocence, her body was made for sin. In the subdued light, her curvaceous silhouette robbed him of breath. With her hair dressed in a simple coiffure, it was the golden lock dangling over her bare shoulder that suggested mischief.

Heaven help him, his wife was stunning.

"Oh, treat us to one of your insightful explanations, Chandler," Mullworth said. "What do they say about a lady who wears red?"

Matthew swallowed down the hard lump in his throat but could do nothing about the swelling in his groin. "They say a woman who wears red craves attention. They say she enjoys teasing men, playing coquette. I say the colour merely reflects an inner passion. It is obvious the lady embodies an inherent feminine appeal and is wearing the dress to give her confidence. I'm in no doubt she has a point to prove."

"You can tell all that from the colour of her gown?" Chigwell said, amazed.

"No. I understand her motives because the lady in red is my wife."

"Well, I'll be damned."

"That lady is your wife?" Parson nudged Matthew's arm. "Lord above, no wonder you've not looked at another woman all evening. And the rumour is you'd married a wallflower. One of those bespectacled sorts who stutters. Damn gossips. One should never believe a word they say."

Chigwell's lips curled up into a lecherous grin. "Now we know why you keep the lady locked in her room."

Matthew stared at the ethereal vision before him. Were he not so bloody annoyed he'd have to fight the urge to gather her up in his arms and take her to bed. Nevertheless, he admired the effort it took for her to appear so self-assured.

Numerous people diverted their gaze to examine the mysterious woman waiting on the stairs. In a matter of seconds, at least one randy lord would prowl through the crowd determined to snare his prey.

"Please forgive me, gentlemen," Matthew said, dismissing the mild sense of panic. "My wife is in need of my company."

Before waiting for a reply, Matthew pushed through the throng. Priscilla witnessed his approach. She bit down on her lip as their gazes locked, but drew on her newfound confidence to raise her chin by way of a challenge. He expected her to walk towards him. But she watched and waited patiently, her magnetic pull drawing him up the five steps.

"Priscilla." He inclined his head, struggled to drag his eyes from the mounds of creamy flesh swelling out of the bodice of her gown. Damn, he'd spent five restless nights picturing their magnificence. "What a pleasant surprise."

"Good evening, Matthew." His wife offered a demure curtsy. "I grew tired of sitting upstairs alone. I thought I would join you for an hour or two."

Licking his dry lips, he scanned her from head to toe. "I feel a compliment is in order. It seems you have the ability to make elegance appear utterly sinful."

She brushed her hands down the front of the velvet gown hugging her body so tight he felt a hint of envy. "You'll be pleased to know I've not spent a penny on my new wardrobe. The dress was kindly donated, and Anne was able to make a few adjustments."

Various emotions fought for supremacy while he considered her delectable form: jealousy, lust, rage. It was a new experience.

"Had you sold the silver to pay for it, I would not have objected."

Despite her beauty, it was the blush rising to her cheeks that made his cock throb.

"So you're not angry that I've come to join the party?"

They'd agreed never to lie. "I'm bloody furious. Indeed, I cannot recall the last time I was so damnably annoyed."

"Is that because I've gone against your wishes," she said boldly, "or are you ashamed of the woman you married?"

"I'm not ashamed of you, Priscilla. That is far from the truth." Indeed, he admired her tenacity. "But you should know I'll not be responsible for my actions should anything untoward happen. The men here are actively looking for their next conquest. They see a married woman as an easy target. And there are some who would relish the chance to declare me a cuckold."

A ghost of a smile touched her lips. "Then you had better make it clear to whom I belong." She peered over his shoulder as the first few strains of a waltz drew couples to the floor. "I assume it is acceptable for the host to dance with his wife."

A man who sought to remain detached from all emotions would refuse, make an excuse. While the waltz provided an opportunity to be close to one's partner, in his house, there were no limitations. To press his body against his wife's voluptuous form would be sheer folly.

Sensing his disquiet she smiled, moved past him and descended the stairs.

"Where are you going?" he demanded.

"I want to dance. As to my choice of partner, well, that decision lies in your hands."

"Priscilla, wait," he whispered through clenched teeth, but the obstinate woman ignored him.

Bloody hell!

So much for her vow to obey.

Though camouflaged amongst the crowd, he knew the ravenous beasts were circling. With no choice but to follow, he caught up with her in a few strides.

As his hand settled on her waist, she swung around to face him. "One dance, Priscilla, and then you must promise to return to your room."

"Two dances, both of them with you, and then I shall leave you to enjoy your night in peace."

Two dances! A saint would struggle to rein in his urges.

"Is that a promise?"

Sapphire-blue eyes sparkled as they searched his face. "It is."

Breathing deeply to dampen his ardour, he held out his hand. She hesitated for a second, no more, and her fingers trembled as she laid her palm on top of his.

Compelled by a sudden urge to claim and conquer, he curled his fingers around her hand and held it tight. He'd sworn to give his protection, and by God he meant it.

"I must warn you," she began as he drew her into the middle of the floor to join the other guests swirling about in perpetual circles. "I lack co-ordination when it comes to moving quickly. No doubt you are just as skilled at dancing as you are most things."

Matthew narrowed his gaze. "Is that an honest assessment of my character?"

"What I know of it, yes."

"Considering the fact I'm in debt to a card sharp I must assume you refer to my ability to rouse a pleasurable response from your lips." He did not want to embarrass her with a more concise description.

"Yes." She nodded. "I'm surprised how quickly my body reacts to your touch. But I wonder, is it like that with everyone?"

Matthew was momentarily stunned by her reply. He scoured his mind in a bid to offer an opinion. The simple answer was no. Women called out his name during the moment of release, they writhed and panted, confessed to feeling a deep sense of satisfaction. Yet never had he felt a genuine connection. Never had he trusted the response he received. Well, not until he'd met Priscilla.

"No. It is not like that with everyone." His blunt reply masked the sudden feeling of trepidation that rocked him to his core.

"I see," she said with a sigh. "No doubt my inexperience ruined the moment. It appears I am easily excited. As I said, I have never had a good sense of rhythm."

To say her candour astounded him was an understatement. "Priscilla, you misunderstand me. Your inexperience did not ruin the moment. It made the moment more pleasurable."

"Oh, but I thought—" She blinked rapidly. "Never mind."

A need to ease her fears took hold.

"And there is certainly nothing wrong with your sense of co-ordination. You dance beautifully."

Wrinkles appeared on the bridge of her nose. "Beautifully is how debutantes dance. I am in a room full of sinners. I want to know how to dance in such a way as to stimulate and excite my partner."

"Your partner?" An odd growl escaped from his lips. "You'll dance with no other man here but me."

A smile touched the corners of her mouth. "Then show me how to excite you."

Devil take him. All this woman had to do was speak to arouse him to the point of no return.

"Priscilla, I'll not—"

"We agreed that everyone would think we were in love. Why are you holding me as if I were an elderly relative who smells of pottage? Hold me like you never want to let me go."

The lady was intent on rousing a response from him. What harm could it do? If everyone could see he loved his wife then perhaps it would make life easier. Lucinda Pearce would graze in pastures new, and it would serve as a warning to those gentlemen who thought to try their luck with the mysterious lady in red.

"If you want excitement, Priscilla, I am more than happy to give it you."

She sucked in a breath. "But I want you to enjoy the experience, too."

"Trust me." He snorted. She had no idea what she was doing to him. "I will."

Without further comment, he pulled her tight to his body until her breasts pressed against his chest. The hand resting on her waist dipped lower, his fingers gliding down to draw her close. Their thighs brushed as he led her around the floor. The rapid turns and twirls caused their breath to come quickly. Their gazes locked.

"Is this exciting enough?" The depth of his arousal was evident in his voice.

"Can we not spin around a little quicker?"

"You prefer fast to slow?" He clenched his jaw as he imagined covering her body and pounding into her again and again.

"I do. I want to feel the blood rush through my veins."

Holy hell!

"Then I suggest you hold on tight." Offering a wicked grin, he swung her around and around. They were completely out of time with the music. No doubt they were attracting attention though he couldn't drag his eyes from hers.

They twirled until they were dizzy. She was so close her breath breezed across his cheek. The smell of roses swamped him. Sweet. Fresh. Stimulating. When she giggled, the sound sent a bolt of desire shooting through his body. His hard cock threatened to tear through the material of his breeches. Had they been alone, he'd have taken her where they stood.

As the last few notes of the waltz played out, they slowed and caught their breath. Her cheeks flushed, her full lips parted. Damn. It would be another two hours before the guests departed. The anticipation of claiming his wife's body would kill him.

"My blood is pumping so fast I can hear it rushing in my ears." Her eyes sparkled with desire. "I feel exhilarated. You really are a remarkable dancer."

"A gentleman is only as good as his partner allows."

"Then together we are both remarkable."

"Indeed."

He took her hand, placed it in the crook of his arm and led her from the floor. "Come. Let me find you some refreshment." He ignored the whispers and odd glances. "I assume you'd prefer our second dance to be a waltz, too."

Holding her close once again would stoke the flames of desire until he could visit her in her bedchamber.

She stopped and turned to face him. "Thank you for dancing with me. It was wonderful. But I shall leave you to your guests."

Disappointment flared in his chest. It was an odd sensation. "I thought we agreed on two dances? Don't you want me to twirl you about the floor?" Lord, he sounded like a disgruntled mistress.

She placed her palm on his chest. "Another time, perhaps. After our scandalous display, I fear I may attract entirely the wrong attention." She smiled. "Good night, Matthew."

Without another word, she mounted the steps and disappeared

out into the hall. He stood there dumbfounded, his mind lost in a cloud of confusion. He caught his footman's attention, nodded by way of a silent order to ensure Priscilla reached her room safely.

Desperate to find a distraction from the clawing need ravaging his body, he returned to Lord Parson and the group of drunken gentlemen.

"Well, well," Parson said with a chuckle, "I doubt there's a man in here who doesn't envy your position. I assume you sent your wife back to the bedchamber before every dissolute sot begs for a place on her dance card."

"After your amorous antics, I'm surprised you've not followed her upstairs," Chigwell added.

Matthew brushed his hand through his hair. The sudden urge to beat the hell out of any man who dared even mention his wife took hold. "What sort of host would I be if I neglected my guests only to serve my own purpose?" When he joined Priscilla in the bedchamber, it would be as her husband, in their home. Not as a libertine with an audience of debauchers.

Parson slapped him on the back. "After such a lively display one thing is certain."

Matthew feigned interest though hoped the fellow was wise enough to guard his damn tongue. "And what is that?"

"The gossips got one thing right. From what I saw, you are definitely in love with your wife."

Lord Parson was mistaken. There was no doubt that he lusted after the lady, but after a lifetime of suppressing all emotion, he lacked the capacity to love.

CHAPTER 9

*W*ith a claw-like grip on the balustrade, Priscilla climbed the stairs to her bedchamber. The slow, hesitant steps were like those of a lady who'd consumed far too much wine. No doubt those passing by would presume her wavering stemmed from an inability to focus.

But her fickle heart proved to be the problem. The organ hammered in her chest as she fought the urge to rush back to the ballroom, to rest her head on Matthew's chest and dance until dawn.

However, one did not win a game with a single hand of cards. And this was a game of skill, not chance. Patience and strength reaped rewards. She had to be the one in control of the play if she had any hope of succeeding.

Priscilla was about to enter her room when a shuffling noise inside captured her attention. She turned and peered over the balustrade, noted the footman, John, had returned to his post at the bottom of the stairs. Should she stumble upon an intruder, one scream and John would be at her side in seconds.

Trembling fingers gripped the brass knob and eased it to the right. But the door was locked. Foolishly, it had not occurred to her to secure the room when she'd ventured downstairs. With some trepidation, she tried it again.

The sound of footsteps padding towards the door forced her to step back.

With her hand clutching her throat, Priscilla noted the faint sliver of light from the room beyond before recognising her maid's fearful face.

"Good Lord, Anne, you frightened me half to death." Priscilla slipped into the room and locked the door behind her. "Why did you not return to your quarters as I instructed? It's not safe to creep around at night when Mr Chandler has visitors."

Despite Anne's reassurances, Priscilla had told the maid to stay in her room below stairs and bolt the door. While Matthew prohibited the guests from entering the servants' quarters, she'd heard enough tales to know there was always one rogue willing to try his luck.

"I knew you'd struggle to undress." Anne's lips formed a thin line. Her pale skin and red hair enhanced her sombre expression. "And I'd finished making the alterations to the blue gown and wanted to show you what I'd done."

Priscilla glanced beyond Anne's shoulder to the sapphire-blue gown laid out on the bed.

"I made the sleeves smaller as you said." Anne scuttled over and held the garment aloft. "I put the black ribbon under the bodice and added the fine layer of matching silk gauze to the skirt."

The next time she felt courageous enough to venture downstairs, the blue gown would be the perfect choice to capture her husband's attention.

Priscilla moved to examine Anne's remarkable work. "You're wasted as a maid. You should have a modiste shop that caters to the elite." Priscilla touched the oval jewel in the centre of the bodice. "What prompted you to add the brooch?"

Anne's green eyes held a hint of mischief. "You ... you

wanted the gown to draw people's attention. The weight of the brooch causes the material to sit lower in the middle of the bosom."

Priscilla's stomach flipped over at the thought of wearing the gown while dancing with Matthew. Would he be just as eager for a second dance, or would her inexperience in seduction leave her floundering?

Nerves pushed to the fore. "I'm so glad you're here. I don't know what I'd do without your help." And Isabella's help, of course.

Anne chuckled. "I'm glad Mr Chandler saw sense. How can he expect a lady to leave her home and not bring her maid?"

When he'd offered marriage, Matthew had not expected to bear the cost of keeping a maid. His reluctance to have another female servant in the house, Priscilla suspected, stemmed from a fear of controlling the licentious nature of his guests.

"Mr Chandler will be furious if he finds you in here tonight, Anne, what with that rowdy rabble downstairs."

"You'll lose a few buttons if you try to undress yourself, and I've laced your stays far too tight."

Priscilla put her hand to her stomach. "Perhaps that's why I've been struggling to breathe." It wasn't. Her husband had the power to empty her lungs with one lingering glance.

"I'll hang the gown in the dressing room and then help you undress."

Priscilla touched Anne's arm. "I don't want Mr Chandler to see it. I want it to be a surprise."

Anne smiled. "I'll put the gown in the armoire. Unlike some of his guests, let's hope Mr Chandler's not of a mind to rummage through a lady's clothes."

"It's not the clothes the guests are interested in."

Chuckling to herself, Anne took the garment and hid it away. She returned to help Priscilla into her nightgown and brush out her hair.

Once ready for bed, Priscilla placed her hand on the maid's arm. "Let me call John to escort you back to your room." With the loud jeers rumbling through the house, she wouldn't rest until Anne was back safely in the servants' quarters.

"There's no need, madam."

Refusing to listen to Anne's protests, Priscilla unlocked the door, called down to the footman and gave her instruction.

"You're to wait with her until she bolts the door. Is that understood?"

A frown marred John's brow. He glanced back over his shoulder. "I'm supposed to watch the stairs, madam."

"I'll hover on the landing and call out should anything untoward happen." Anger flared. "Heavens, I should not have to worry about being accosted in my home."

Surely there was a better way to supplement one's income. Regardless of Uncle Henry's preaching to the contrary, some things were more important than money. Once he'd paid the gambling debt, Matthew should think about hiring premises for his select gatherings.

Armed with a vase, Priscilla hid in the shadows until John returned to his post. He nodded up to her and gave a reassuring smile before turning to block the staircase.

Well, one thing was certain, Priscilla thought as she returned to her room and locked the door, anxiety had a way of dampening one's ardour.

Picking up the key to the connecting door from the side table, she strode into the dressing room. Dismissing all doubts, she thrust the key into the lock and turned it until she heard the click.

Most women would say it was wrong to shut one's husband out. Indeed, if Matthew did not attempt to enter her room tonight, their marriage was doomed to fail. Lacking the skill and knowledge necessary, she could do nothing more to seduce him. But he could not pick her up and put her down when it suited him. Such a one-sided relationship would chip away at her confidence, leave a constant feeling of inadequacy.

With a resolute sigh, she returned to her chamber, placed the key on the dressing table out of reach and blew out the candles.

Despite sliding in between warm sheets, she had no hope of sleeping. There were too many chaotic thoughts whizzing about in her head. Would she hear Matthew rattle the door? As her husband, would he demand access to her room, to her body? It didn't help that she caught a whiff of his masculine scent wafting in the air. Bergamot and some sort of spice. Her imagination had the power to perform the conjurer's trick just to tempt and tease.

A long, anxious hour passed.

Desperate to find a distraction, she moved to the window to observe the drunken revellers making too much noise in the garden. Two men were standing back-to-back on the lawn, their fingers forming the shape of a pistol raised in front of their face.

"The lady calls the winner," one gentleman shouted.

The woman spectating braced her hands on her hips and counted. The fools trudged forward in opposite directions, turned on the count of ten and pretended to fire their fake weapons. As though taking a shot to the chest, both men fell to the floor. They lay on the grass, their eyes closed, their bodies still. The lady put her hand to her mouth as she examined both victims, patting each one on the thighs, daring to massage and cup the bulge between their legs. Unable to contain his excitement as the woman fiddled and fondled, one man opened his eyes and groaned.

"You lose, Malcolm." The woman jumped up, ran over to congratulate the other contestant who was remarkably skilful at playing a corpse.

Was it only dissolute men who liked these sorts of games? Perhaps she should think of a game to play with Matthew. Something wicked, sinful, something to heat the blood.

She watched from the window as the winning gentleman dragged the woman away to the bushes to claim his prize. After her waltz with Matthew, she understood the need to rouse lust in a man. But lust was easily sated. A woman needed to woo a man with more than her body.

Priscilla returned to her bed. If the flurry of illicit activities in the garden were anything to go by, the party would soon be at an end.

Recalling Isabella's comments about the three steps to love, she spent another hour ignoring shrieks and banging doors to concentrate on her plans for tomorrow.

The sound of raised voices travelled up from the hall. Deep, masculine chuckles were interspersed with a string of incoherent sentences. In the distance, the rumble of carriage wheels on the cobblestones convinced her the guests were departing.

It would not be long now.

After a period of constant noise that left a thrumming in her ears, the house fell silent.

The trudge of footsteps on the stairs and the creak of floor-boards on the landing alerted her to Matthew's presence. At least he'd not gone out on another one of his mysterious appointments. Many London streets were unsafe in the daytime let alone in the dark. Only a few nights ago a gentleman was mugged at knife-point after being forced out of his conveyance by a broken carriage wheel.

As she strained to listen out for his movements, the silence proved deafening. In the end, she crept into the dressing room and pressed her ear to the connecting door.

Matthew was pacing about in his chamber. The clink of crystal led her to conclude he kept a decanter of liquor by his bed. Perhaps the effort it took to entertain scoundrels took its toll.

A loud sigh forced her to her knees to peer through the keyhole. Though the room was dimly lit, she could see him sitting on the edge of the bed, well, one half of him. He downed what was left of the amber liquid in the glass and placed the vessel on the floor before tugging on his cravat. Pulling the material from around his neck, he threw it onto the bed. The waistcoat soon followed, along with his stockings and shoes. Jumping to his feet, he dragged his shirt from his breeches so it hung loose.

Priscilla pressed her eye closer to the keyhole, but it wasn't the cold draught breezing through that forced her to draw back. Matthew had dragged his shirt over his head to reveal his muscular torso.

Heavens.

Her heart hammered against her ribs.

The desire to see more left her salivating. The pulsing sensation between her legs grew, and she feared she was too weak to refuse this man anything.

This simply would not do, yet it didn't stop her looking again.

With his breeches hanging low on his hips, he padded towards the dressing room. Priscilla shot up and shuffled back. A second felt longer than an hour. Mouth open, she stared at the door. Watching. Waiting. The brass knob moved a fraction to the right but was accompanied by a loud thud and mumbled curse.

"Bloody hell."

Expecting the door to be unlocked, he'd obviously thought to march right in.

The knob rattled. Once. Twice. The third time he rapped on the wooden panel.

"Priscilla."

There was a moment of silence.

"Priscilla. Open the door."

The pulsing in her throat almost choked her. Anticipating the betrayal of her trembling fingers, she clenched them into fists.

"Damn it, Priscilla." He knocked loudly this time. "Damnation. The woman teases me and then falls asleep." His irate mutterings were audible.

When he opened his bedchamber door and marched along the landing, she knew he would knock again. Slipping back into her room, she flopped down onto the bed.

He tried the knob on her door. Lord knows why as he was the one who insisted she lock it. "Priscilla. It's me. Open the door before I wake the household."

Priscilla covered her mouth with her hand. Part of her craved his attention, longed to touch him. If she let him in, the experience was sure to be the most pleasurable of her life. Her breasts grew heavy at the thought of taking him into her willing body.

With one last knock, he stomped back along the corridor.

Disappointment flared but was soon replaced with an immense sense of satisfaction. He wanted her. By some miraculous feat, she had seduced her husband. When she did decide to let him into her bed, she would have to make the moment memorable.

But she couldn't worry about that now.

Tomorrow, she would use what she had learnt from Isabella to entice him further. Perhaps she might give a little of herself if it meant discovering more about him. Of course, she couldn't leave him frustrated for too long. No doubt Lucinda Pearce was lurking in the background waiting for an opportune moment to pounce.

CHAPTER 10

*T*he slivers of light streaming through the gap in the curtains should have given Matthew a renewed sense of optimism for a brighter day. But a throbbing erection had robbed him of a pleasant night's sleep.

Waking to a solid cock was not a new experience. It was his body's way of reminding him everything was working as it ought. Usually, it proved to be a nuisance. What was the point when he had no one to share it with? Though if relief was what he wanted, he could always beat the devil, as they say.

His thoughts drifted to the woman who occupied the next bedchamber, to the image of him rattling the blasted dressing room door to gain entrance. Why the hell had he given her the damn key? From the moment he'd taken her in his arms and waltzed about the floor, he'd been desperate to bury himself inside her. Surely she knew. Perhaps her inexperience with men meant she'd failed to read the signs.

Bloody hell!

While he expected to receive pleasure from the marriage bed, he'd not expected to lust after his wife. Of course, it was only to sate a physical need. The few nights where he'd fought the urge to take her without being encumbered by clothing, helped to rid him of that slight sense of desperation—or so he'd thought.

A light rap on the door brought his valet, Lawson. With his robust frame and expressionless face, the man would be better suited in the role of executioner. Lawson doubled as a deterrent at parties, patrolled the house glaring at guests with his cold black eyes.

Matthew stretched his arms above his head. "What time is it?"

Lawson poured the water from the pitcher into the bowl on the washstand. "It's a little after ten, sir. Will you want to eat in your room? I can have a tray brought up."

Ten. Excellent. The lady of the house followed a strict routine in the mornings.

"There's no need. I shall join Mrs Chandler in the dining room." As soon as the blood filling his nether regions decided it was better served elsewhere.

Besides, he wanted the key to the dressing room and would broach the subject whilst casually sipping coffee and nibbling on toast and jam.

Lawson cleared his throat. "Mrs Chandler rose early this morning and has gone out."

"Out?" Was the woman intent on ruining all of his plans? "Where the hell has she gone at this hour?" He'd not meant to take his frustration out on his valet.

"From what I understand, Mrs Chandler likes to ride in the park."

Matthew sat bolt upright. "At ten o'clock in the morning?"

The rogues who attended his gatherings were just as likely to accost her outdoors during the day. After witnessing her wrapped seductively in her red velvet dress, there were bound to be men eager to offer a proposition. He dragged his hand down his face and groaned. Devil take him. When he'd offered his hand, he'd not expected to feel an overwhelming urge to protect her.

The lady was proving to be far too distracting.

"I believe Mrs Chandler likes to feel the wind in her hair and thought she would have more privacy in the park if she left at nine. Hopkins asked me to inform you that she has taken the white mare. As it has been some time since she's ridden, Billings suggested it was the wisest choice."

The hair at his nape prickled to attention. "Please tell me she has not gone out alone." Nothing surprised him when it came to Priscilla, but he hoped his staff had more sense. "Did no one think to inform me sooner?"

Lawson frowned. "Usually after a night spent entertaining you insist no one disturbs you before ten."

"Yes, but that was before my wife wreaked havoc with my routine."

Why could she not spend her days practising the pianoforte, working on her embroidery frame, visiting other ladies eager to talk about their mundane tasks? Why was it that, despite rousing anger, her spontaneous impulses excited him?

"Billings sent Pike to accompany her," Lawson said, "though he's the only groom I've ever seen who looks cumbersome on a horse. As such he's sure to attract a few gapes and stares."

"That's because his arms are larger than a typical man's thighs." The news that Pike rode with Priscilla eased Matthew's fears somewhat. "Well, I suppose there's one consolation. He hits harder than anyone I've ever fought at Jackson's."

"A man like that has his uses. I was glad of his assistance during the fight in the mews last month," Lawson replied as he laid out the shaving implements with such care and attention one would think they were priceless jewels. "As Mrs Chandler is out, do you still wish to take your meal downstairs?"

How long did it take to ride in the park? An hour—two at most?

"Yes. By the time I'm washed and dressed, Mrs Chandler should be home." When she found him sitting alone, she was bound to feel an ounce of guilt. Consequently, she would be inclined to give him the key to the connecting door.

"If you have no preference regarding your attire, may I suggest the yellow waistcoat with the midnight-blue coat, sir?"

Damn. He'd not suffer the embarrassment of informing his valet he'd been locked out of the dressing room. Besides, for Priscilla to feel any remorse did he not need to appear somewhat solemn? Yellow simply wouldn't do. But then it was not pity he wanted her to feel in her breast.

"On second thoughts, just hand me my silk robe. I shall eat in here. When Mrs Chandler returns, send her up at once."

Lawson inclined his head and retrieved the burgundy dressing gown from the chair. "Shall I leave it on the bed, sir, or do you require assistance?"

"Leave it on the bed." Matthew had no problem with nudity but would rather not flaunt his engorged manhood. He would have to conjure a repulsive image in order to deal with the problem. To be in a state of arousal would not serve him well when dealing with Priscilla.

The small hand on the mantel clock had moved past eleven when he heard the light rap at his bedchamber door. Matthew was sitting on top of the coverlet, his robe gaping at the chest but covering his modesty, his breakfast laid out on a tray in front of him. The toast in the rack was as cold and hard as stone. The tea in the pot had stewed and resembled runny gravy.

"Come in." He buttered a slab of toast with feigned enthusiasm.

The door eased away from the jamb. Priscilla peered inside. "Hopkins said you wished to see me."

"Come in and close the door." It took a tremendous effort not to gag as he bit into the bread and it crumbled in his mouth. "Lawson informed me you were out riding in the park."

She slipped inside and closed the door. "I rode along the Ladies' Mile, observed the fallow deer in the Pound." A chuckle escaped from her lips. "It's so fresh out this morning. I could have stayed in the park for hours, but Pike is not easy company."

A ruby glow coloured her cheeks. Her blue eyes sparkled with a vitality that stole his breath.

"Pike can be rather solemn and not very personable. But he's loyal and takes his responsibilities seriously. Next time, I might join you. I can't remember the last time I rode in the morning."

What was he thinking? He detested riding.

She stepped further into the room. "There is nothing like an early morning ride to get the blood pumping."

"I couldn't agree more."

"It really sets you up for the day."

"That has been my experience." He noted the outdated style of her faded blue riding habit. A sudden desire to lavish her with gifts took hold. "I'm told it's been a while since you rode. Perhaps you should order a new habit. Something a little brighter. Something to reflect your sunny disposition."

A smile lit up her face but quickly faded. "Under the circumstances, it would be unwise to be frivolous." She brushed the sleeves of her coat. "This will be fine for now."

Matthew considered the woman before him. Most ladies of his acquaintance would not refuse the offer of new clothes. They had no care where the money came from to fund their extravagant tastes. Nothing was more important than being seen in fashionable garments. His wife was not so shallow. His wife saw their marriage as a partnership. Once he'd repaid the vowel and implemented his plan to beat the card sharps, he would give her everything she needed and more.

"You do not desire a new riding habit?" He was keen to understand her reasoning.

She shrugged. "I would like to believe I am not so vain as to put financial pressure on my family merely to satisfy a whim."

The word *family* prickled like pins digging into his shoulders. In his experience, family were not to be trusted.

"Indeed." He pushed the tray away and moved to sit on the edge of the bed. "May I ask you a question?"

Her gaze journeyed southward over his robe, lingered on his bare legs. Pushing two fingers down between the ruffled blouse and her throat, she sucked in a breath.

Matthew suppressed a grin though he felt like a disgruntled mistress using every tactic possible to secure a lover's attention.

"You're my husband. You may ask me anything you like."

"And you'll answer honestly?"

She folded her arms across her chest. "Of course. Does truthfulness not form the basis of our marriage?"

For nigh on twenty years, Matthew's family had branded him a liar. He knew what he'd seen that day in the forest. But it was easier to forsake a small boy than ruin reputations. Consequently, Priscilla had no idea what hearing the truth meant to him.

Matthew shook the memory away, forced himself to concentrate on the woman before him.

"*Vain* is the last word I would use to describe you," he said as an unexpected feeling of admiration filled his chest. "So I am curious to know what prompted you to come downstairs last night. What prompted you to dress in such a way as to secure every man's attention?"

There was a brief silence as she nibbled her bottom lip and her chest rose and fell rapidly. It took tremendous strength of character to be candid. Would she falter?

"My only objective was to secure your attention." From her firm jaw, he knew the words had been difficult to say. "I have no interest in any other man."

"Then you must know you succeeded."

Despite pursing her lips, she could not hide the glimmer of satisfaction. "I hoped as much."

"Then why lock the connecting door between our rooms? Surely you knew I would visit you in your chamber."

Silence ensued.

"Be honest with me," he persisted.

"It will be difficult for you to understand. I do not think or feel the same way you do. I struggle to separate the physical and emotional." From the way she moistened her lips, he knew she wanted him, even now. But she stepped back towards the door. "I need more time to harden my heart. It would be foolish to fall in love with you."

"Why?" His instant reply confused even him. They were the last words he wanted to hear from anyone's lips.

A frown marred her brow. "Can you imagine what it would be like to love someone, to give everything of yourself and know those feelings will never be returned?" With a little shake of the head, her hand settled on the doorknob. "As your wife, I will welcome you into my bed, Matthew. But I ask that you be patient with me. I like you. I enjoy your company and hope you can learn to like me equally."

Well, he'd asked for honesty, and she'd given it to him.

The problem was he didn't know what to make of it. What had he expected? Did he want her to see the act as merely a job, her duty? Did he think a woman brimming with virtue would lie with him like a whore each night?

"I shall leave you to your breakfast." She was already halfway out of the door. "I'm to meet Isabella at noon. She is visiting the modiste and requires my opinion on her new wardrobe. After-wards, I may call on my aunt to see how she fares."

He nodded, his mind still somewhat jumbled. "Will you be home for dinner?"

"If I said yes would we be dining together?"

"Of course." He had to go out later in the evening though it would be the last time he visited the gaming hells. After two weeks spent investigating the methods the sharps used to deceive their opponents, he had almost cracked the codes.

"Then I shall see you this evening." She slipped out into the hall and closed the door.

Minutes passed before he moved.

For days he'd imagined settling between his wife's cushioned thighs and thrusting home. The thought kept him in a constant state of semi-arousal. The irony of their situation was that he'd needed time to adjust, too. He did not want to feel any attachment; he did not want to feel anything other than lust. Most men in his situation would bed her, regardless. The women he'd had in the past always appreciated his skill for giving pleasure. Just because Priscilla was his wife why should it be any different?

But then realisation dawned.

The truth knocked him back like a kick to the gut. His obsession with honesty was the problem. Other women had wanted nothing but his cock. He'd wanted nothing but to satisfy an urge. There had been no expectations, just an honest arrangement.

But things were different now.

Priscilla needed more than the use of his body. His disdain for lies and falsehoods would make him a hypocrite if he tried to ignore her wishes.

Damnation. It was all a bloody mess. His time would be better spent plotting revenge on the card sharps than fantasising about bedding his wife.

CHAPTER 11

The instruction to meet Matthew for a pre-dinner drink in the drawing room took Priscilla by surprise. After revealing she was in danger of falling in love, his desire to spend more time together was the last thing she expected.

Drawing in a deep breath, she pushed at the half-open door. Matthew was lounging on the sofa, legs stretched out in front and crossed at the ankles. The spicy scent of cologne in the air teased her nostrils. His intoxicating smell brought to mind passionate kisses in the carriage; the masculine taste had coated her lips for hours.

Upon noting her arrival, Matthew jumped up. Penetrating emerald eyes scanned her plain muslin dress, a garment far removed from the vibrant gown she'd worn to the party. But there were many facets to her character. One dress did not define her.

"Were you expecting me to wear something more fetching?"

"Not at all." The corner of his mouth curled up. "Where you're concerned, I would not make the mistake of presuming anything."

The comment made her sound impulsive, daring, those qualities necessary to excite a man. If only it were true. "Someone once said that a person's outward appearance often reflects their inner thoughts. One's choice of clothes can convey mood and purpose."

"Based on what I know of your character, I would agree." His inquisitive gaze scrutinised her from head to toe. "Last night you were a woman intent on seduction. Every delicious element conveyed strength and determination. Tonight, you are the natural, unassuming woman whose life is entwined with mine."

As always, his response was insightful.

"And which one do you prefer?"

"Both, for together they make for an interesting combination."

A sudden fluttering filled her chest. "Unlike us, most married couples spend time together before deciding to wed. They learn of each other's likes and dislikes, appreciate the similarities, respect the differences." She was growing accustomed to speaking so candidly. "We've been swept up in a whirlwind and must find a way to muddle through."

"I know it's a cliché, but things will become easier over time. Equally, every minute should be enjoyed and savoured."

How close would they be a year from now? Would they still be lovers? Would the excitement she felt today be something more profound tomorrow? Perhaps she'd made a mistake telling him she intended to harden her heart.

Priscilla sighed. "Worrying about the future can ruin the present. Sometimes I think too much, panic about how things should be. But I expect nothing from you other than your friendship and support."

Guilt flared. It wasn't the whole truth.

"I have the utmost regard for your opinion, even if it highlights my weaknesses." He gestured to the decanters on the side table. "What would you like to drink? Instincts say pour you a sherry, but I suspect I am far from the mark."

"Sherry is often too sweet, but a nip of brandy will suffice. Uncle Henry believes buying sherry for ladies is a waste of good money. He believes we should all stick to drinking tea. Yet having learnt of his penchant for gambling, I'm convinced it has something to do with not paying his bills."

"No doubt you're right." Matthew moved to the drinks table, pulled the crystal stopper from the decanter and poured two glasses of brandy. "Lord Callan's solicitor is yet to contact me about payment of your dowry."

"Well, I'd like to say that such things take time to arrange." Doubt surfaced. "But I fear he may be stalling. Will it be a problem?"

Matthew returned, glasses in hand. Priscilla's fingers brushed his as she took the drink. The frisson of awareness she'd felt on that first night in the garden returned.

"I hope not." He raised his glass in salute. "To muddling through."

"To muddling through."

Their gazes locked over the rim of the glass as she sipped the brandy. The fiery liquid warmed her chest although she suspected the spirit had nothing to do with the heat building between her thighs.

"Was there a reason you wanted to meet in here before dinner?" The question had plagued her for an hour or more. The soothing effects of the brandy gave her the courage to ask.

"It seems we have reached a knot in the thread, so to speak, and must work to unravel it if we have any hope of moving forward. This morning you said you liked me and enjoyed my company. I feel the same way about you. Perhaps building a solid friendship is a good place to start."

Priscilla's heart swelled. "People will chastise us for our modern way of thinking. Most married couples lead separate lives. Well, except for Tristan and Isabella."

Two lines appeared between his brows. "Do you regret the decision you made in Holbrook's garden? Tristan would have done the honourable thing. He would have forsaken his own happiness to save your reputation."

She did not need to consider the question. "Tristan is like a brother. Any physical relationship would have been impossible. Ruination was the only option had you not played the hero."

His expression darkened. "I am far from a hero."

"You have never lied to me, Matthew. That is one quality of a hero. I know why you married me—to save your friend, to save yourself and to help me, too. It might not qualify as heroic, but it was not an entirely selfish decision."

"There was another reason." His heated gaze fell to her lips. "It is only right you know the truth about the man you married. Friends don't lie, and so I ask you to forgive my bluntness. I married you because I wanted to bed you. I wanted to pleasure you until your innocent mouth begged to be fucked."

This time his honesty stole her breath. "Well! Heavens!" She swallowed. "Now I know why you rattled the door fifteen times or more last night." One had to find amusement in the situation.

He narrowed his gaze. "Damn. So you were awake. Do you know what it's like to lie in bed all night with a throbbing erection?"

"Thankfully, no."

He was silent for a moment. "Do you think me disrespectful for speaking so crudely? I fear it stems from spending too much time with reprobates."

"Thankfully, no. While your words lack sentiment, I appreciate there is a compliment within them somewhere."

Slapping a hand to his chest, he laughed. "So now it is clear we share a mutual appreciation, it would be nice if we could be a little more at ease when together."

The conversation *had* helped to clear the air.

"Perhaps we should work backwards—"

"It's my favourite position."

"Must every conversation revert to your antics in the bedchamber?"

"Forgive me, please continue."

"I meant we should get to know one another, learn what the other likes and dislikes. For instance, I like picnics and feeling the wind blow my hair. I enjoy sucking the juice from strawberries, laughing until my stomach hurts. Now, what about you?"

"For fear of the conversation following the usual thread, I shall refrain from telling you what I like. Perhaps at some point in the future, I may be lucky enough to demonstrate."

Priscilla brought the glass to her lips and gave a coy smile. "You might."

"Is that a promise?"

"Not quite."

Matthew drained what was left of the brandy in his glass. "I have an idea how to please you."

"Just one? Are you not known for your prowess in the bedchamber? Has your appetite for carnal pleasures been exaggerated?"

"There is only one way to find out." He arched a brow. "Put me to the test."

No doubt he would always have the upper hand when it came to banter. "You can start by telling me your idea."

"To prove you right, and support the theory that I'm not entirely selfish, I shall tailor the evening around the things you like."

She liked a great many things she'd not mentioned. The taste of brandy on his lips. The way his tongue danced with hers to send shocks shooting to her core.

"Forgive me for pointing out the obvious, but isn't it rather late for a picnic?"

"Not at all. It's only late if one wants to sit in the park." A mischievous glint sparkled in his eyes. "Wait here. I'll be back in a moment."

Thrusting the empty glass into her hand, he marched from the room.

While waiting, Priscilla placed the empty glasses on the table. She contemplated refilling them though it would not be wise for her to drink much more. Her husband possessed a charismatic charm she found highly addictive. It took a tremendous effort not to strip to her chemise and surrender her body. She was heading into dangerous territory. The desire to place his needs above her own was fast becoming a priority.

The sudden commotion in the hall diverted her attention. Matthew entered the drawing room, held open the door for two footmen carrying a low table.

"Place it in the centre of the room, on top of the rug." Matthew pointed to the exact position. "Bring a cloth, cutlery, and serve the dishes on smaller platters."

Numerous servants bustled in and out, set about laying the table and transporting their meal from the kitchen.

Hopkins appeared at the door. "Is everything to your satisfaction, sir?"

Matthew scanned the array of delectable dishes: fish, asparagus tart, a terrine of some sort, the quantity far too much for two people. "We're just missing the bowl of strawberries."

"That might prove to be a problem," Hopkins said with a hint of remorse. "Cook had not factored strawberries into the week's menu."

Matthew's shoulders sagged. "Can you not find some from somewhere?"

Hopkins grimaced. "What with the hour being late …"

"Never mind," she said. Matthew's eagerness to please touched her. The thoughtful gesture was enough. "We'll save the strawberries for another time."

Hopkins inclined his head. "Is there anything else you need?"

"No, we shall serve ourselves. I'll inform you once we've finished." Matthew stepped outside with Hopkins, returned a moment later and closed the door. "Your picnic, my lady." With an air of smug satisfaction, he gestured to the table.

"Are we to sit on the floor?" Excitement bubbled in her belly at the thought of such unconventional behaviour.

"Is that not what people do on picnics?"

Priscilla stepped onto the Persian rug, but Matthew came forward and caught her wrist.

"There is just one more thing to do before we eat," he said, threading his fingers into her hair. His head was so close his warm breath breezed across her cheek. With nimble fingers, he removed the pins slowly. One at a time. Golden locks tumbled around her shoulders, and he teased them loose, brushed a few tendrils from her face. "I can't promise you'll feel the wind blowing your hair, but hopefully you'll feel a similar sense of freedom."

A strange ache filled her chest: a yearning she had never experienced before. It took all the effort she possessed not to throw her arms around his neck and plunder his mouth.

"Are you attempting to seduce me?"

He brushed her cheek with the backs of his fingers. "Only if it's working."

It was working.

"Do you think it is?"

A sinful smile touched his lips. "Well, I hear the hitch in your breath. I see the glazed look of desire swimming in your eyes. You've moistened your lips too many times to count." He trailed his fingers from her shoulder down the front of her dress. "I could offer a host of other observations, but I fear my licentious banter will ruin the moment."

Priscilla swallowed in an attempt to gather her wits. Everything he said was true. But she would not surrender without gaining something in return.

"You enjoy a wager," she said, for it would not do to appear too eager. "Do you feel confident enough to gamble?"

Matthew drew his head back, wide eyes conveying his surprise at the challenge. "What did you have in mind?"

"While we eat, we will play a game. We could draw cards. The winner of each hand can demand something from the other." She would use the opportunity to find out more about him. Where did he go on those nightly outings? Why did he distance himself from his family? Had Lucinda Pearce approached him again? "And the loser must comply."

A snigger burst from his lips. "If I win, you do know what I'll want as my prize."

"Of course. You will want to pleasure me until I beg to be … now, what was that delightful word you used?"

"I shall refrain from using the obscenity in your presence again." He folded his arms across his chest. "You won't beat me. I may have been duped by sharps, but I have some skill for cards."

Priscilla shrugged. "It will be a game of chance. No one can predict the outcome."

"Trust me, love. I'm not leaving this room until I've claimed your body."

In that regard, she had nothing to lose, everything to gain. Of course, it helped that she had an excellent memory and could recall every card previously played.

"Then pray Fate is on your side." Fate owed her something for her plight.

Perhaps her luck was about to change.

CHAPTER 12

*A*s a man who found most people predictable, and whose expectations were rarely challenged, he had to admit his wife surprised him at every turn. How was it possible to convey innocence while employing the skills of a temptress?

Are you attempting to seduce me?

Her words echoed in his ears. The situation was laughable. The only person being seduced was him. Inside, his blood pumped like that of a boisterous pup, desperate to paw her, nip and lick, to get her to stroke him—to capture her attention.

"Shall we take our seats?" His confident tone conveyed nothing of his internal struggle. Tugging on the drawer of the rosewood dresser, he removed a pack of playing cards. "I'm eager to begin our little game."

With a playful smirk, she slipped off her slippers and sat on the floor in front of the low table. "To make it fair, we should fill our plates with food. After each mouthful, we will play one hand. The game will not finish until we've eaten our meal. That way it will prevent the urge to rush ahead."

After removing his coat and throwing it onto the chair, he sat at the opposite side of the table. "You ask to dance quickly, play cards slowly. A man is left dizzy trying to work out what you want."

"It is simple." She ran the tips of her fingers across her collarbone. "While we all crave a thrill, some things are best savoured."

Bloody hell!

The woman teased him to the point of madness.

"Then you should prepare yourself, for I guarantee you'll experience both sensations this evening."

"Only if you win," Priscilla countered.

"Despite all my honest protestations, I am prepared to cheat to secure a night with you."

"Perhaps I know a few tricks myself." The blush colouring her cheeks restored his masculine pride, but there was nothing timid about her response. "Overconfidence is often one's downfall."

Damn the food and card game. He wanted this woman now.

"But as I trust you," she continued. "You can shuffle the deck and deal the cards."

Matthew snorted. "You trust a man who admits he's selfish?"

"I trust a man whose integrity speaks for itself."

He stared at her, unsure how to respond to the compliment. To fill the silence, he picked up the silver serving utensils and selected a piece of tart, a slice of duck terrine, roast pork, French beans. "Did you have a particular game in mind?"

Priscilla followed his lead, taking small portions and arranging the food neatly on her plate. "We'll play twenty-one but follow the basic rules."

"Twenty-one? Do you think it a game of chance?"

"It's a game of luck that requires an element of risk and some skill." She inhaled deeply. "Now, as in all card games, we must reveal the stakes before we play the hand. If I win, I want you to tell me about Lucinda Pearce."

The mere mention of the courtesan's name made his skin crawl. How the hell did she know of Lucinda? "I have nothing to hide. If you want to know about Miss Pearce you only need ask. But, if we are starting with small wagers then you can tell me why you agreed to marry me."

"Done." Offering a curt nod, she dug her fork into an oyster, covered it with her lips and pulled it into her mouth.

To suppress all rampant thoughts, Matthew cleared a space in front of them, shuffled the cards, dealt two each and placed the rest of the pack face down.

"Would you care for another card?" His heart thumped wildly in his chest as she examined her cards and placed them down on the table. "Or are you happy with your hand?"

"I'll take one more card."

With the tips of his fingers, Matthew pushed the card across the table.

A smile touched her lips as she lifted the corner. "I'm happy with what I have."

His cards amounted to eighteen. Excitement flashed in her eyes as he revealed his hand, and so there was no option but to take another card. He drew a five. "That means I'm out."

Arching a brow, she declared a ten, four and three. "I had seventeen."

Matthew chuckled. "Never trust a woman with the face of an angel. What would you like to know about Lucinda?"

She tapped her finger to her lips. "I know you've shared her bed before. But despite her apparent efforts, I'm confident you do not intend to do so again. Even so, I wonder if the feelings you had are different to those you had when bedding me."

Matthew swallowed. Once again, he had underestimated her skill in combat. In truth, the scenarios were vastly different though he had no notion why.

"Yes, there is a disparity." Without time to analyse his thoughts, he had no option but to be vague. "Perhaps it has something to do with the fact we're married."

The colour drained from her face, and she flinched at his

response. "You mean the act is not as exciting when shackled to the same woman for life."

Matthew frowned. "You misunderstand me. My chest is like a hollow cavern when I think of bedding Lucinda. I lack interest and enthusiasm for the task. When I think of bedding you, every nerve in my body sparks to life." Whatever it all meant, he hoped the explanation placated her. "Does that answer your question?"

"In a way." She picked up the fork and glanced down at the plate. This time she cut the corner off the asparagus tart and ate it slowly before dabbing her mouth with a napkin. "While you finish what you're eating, I'll tell you what we're playing for next. If I win, I want you to tell me about your dreams and aspirations."

Disappointment flared.

The information was hardly a secret. Perhaps nerves prevented her from raising the stakes. "If I win, I want your dress. Just so you're aware, each hand I win will result in me taking another item of clothing until you're down to your chemise."

Dainty fingers flew to her mouth to cover her open lips. "But I'll catch my death of cold."

"Then I'll stoke the fire."

"Are you speaking literally or metaphorically?"

He offered a mischievous grin. "Both."

A nervous energy filled the air. "Then it seems I win regardless of the outcome."

Matthew dealt the cards. Priscilla examined her hand. If a frown and pursed lips conveyed the state of play, the next card could see her out of the game. But was it her intention to deceive?

Her failure to ask for another card confirmed his theory.

To win, he needed luck, not skill. With a knave and a ten, he took a chance it would be enough.

"It's time to reveal your hand, Priscilla."

With a look of suspicion marring her brow she turned over the cards. "I have nineteen."

A rush of satisfaction swept through him though he tried to disguise his elation. In his mind, he said a silent prayer to Fate.

"I win." He flipped his cards over. "I think you'll find that's twenty." Arrogance dripped from every word. He would take immense pleasure undressing his bride.

Without a word, Priscilla jumped up. "Then you will want your prize." Her hands snaked around her back to fiddle with the buttons.

"Allow me." Matthew stood and covered the distance between them in two long, eager strides. His fingers tingled at the prospect of removing a layer of material. With a little more luck, soon there would be nothing but a thin chemise to hide her modesty.

"Under the circumstances is it not wise to lock the door?" There was a nervous edge to her tone, mingled with a hint of excitement.

"No one will disturb us."

He came behind her, undid the row of buttons, smoothed his hands along her shoulders as the garment slithered to the floor. Of course, he had no option but to touch her body as he set about his ministrations.

"I wouldn't worry about the cold." His hand settled on her hip. "The warmth of your skin radiates through the fabric. I'm so hot I'm inclined to remove a few layers myself."

She sucked in a breath. "I am at a rather unfair advantage. But the game is far from over. I believe it's time for food."

They settled back at the table, but he struggled to focus on anything other than the mounds of creamy-white flesh bursting out of her undergarments. He imagined her nipples to be a pretty shade of pink and easily teased to peak. Damn, they'd been married for days, and still he'd not feasted his eyes on them.

"You're right," he said after swallowing a mouthful of game pie. "It seems frightfully unfair of me to claim such a monumental prize."

"Does that mean you intend to remove your shirt?"

"No. But I shall grant your wish. You asked about my dreams and aspirations. I love to paint, landscapes mainly. Were money not a factor I would like to have a studio, somewhere quiet and peaceful where I could spend my days lost in creating beautiful scenes."

A look of wonder illuminated her face. "But surely there is time to paint and host parties? Could you not have a studio here and work during the day?"

"This may sound strange, but creativity requires a clear mind not one encumbered by the negative influences of my guests. The air here is tainted. I've tried to focus many times but to no avail."

"I would love to see your work."

The cruel taunts and jibes of his peers drifted into his mind. In truth, the hostile reaction he'd experienced as a young man played its part in stifling him, too.

"Perhaps when I have a studio, maybe even a patron, then I will show you."

She pursed her lips for a long time. "When my parents died, I imagined a place in my mind where I might visit them. If I followed the path through the forest, I would find a cottage. They were always inside, happy, together. They would hug me and tell me all was well and I would leave them and return to the real world. I visit them often." She gave an odd little wave. "What I mean is you can create the ideal studio in your mind. Every day when you wake you can go there."

As Matthew listened to her wise words, an odd feeling enveloped him—one of admiration, respect, something else, too. Something too complicated to define.

"How can I concentrate when my time is spent thinking of new ways to entertain the dissolute?" It was an excuse. Avoidance was the best technique when dealing with any unwarranted emotion. "I struggle to focus on anything else."

"Then let me help you with your parties. I might not have the skills necessary to please libertines, but there must be some tasks I can attend to."

The strange feeling was there again, swelling, pushing at his ribcage.

"I'll consider the offer. But for now we have a game to finish."

"There is no point asking what you're playing for. If I win, you can tell me where you go on your nightly appointments."

Again, he would have told her had she asked. "Perhaps we should improve the odds of success."

"How so?"

"What about a trade? The answer in return for your petticoat. Our food is cold, and there is every chance we'll be here all night. Patience is not a virtue I aspire to master."

A coy smile touched her lips. "Agreed." She stood, undid the three little buttons on the back and pushed the cotton straps from her shoulders. The garment fell to the floor, and she picked it up and handed it to him.

The petticoat smelt of roses and the unique feminine scent that clung to her skin, yet he resisted the urge to bury his face in the material and inhale deeply.

"For two weeks, I've been touring the gaming hells," he said. "There are three men involved in the card scam. Mr Parker-Brown, Lord Lawrence Boden and Mr Justin Travant." The last gentleman named had not been seen about town in recent weeks. "The men communicate via a complex system of gestures and signals. I have been following their progress, making notes, deciphering the language. Tonight, I intend to observe them at play to test my theory. After that, well, I shall play one more game with the intention of taking back what they stole."

"Tonight? You're going to a gaming hell this evening?"

"I've no choice. Their substantial win at Lord Holbrook's party attracted too much attention. They have since taken to using their skills for deception in the backstreet establishments."

"Do women visit these hells?"

Did Priscilla not trust him?

"Some." They were mostly the ladies of the demi-monde. Women who'd lost favour. The wives of scoundrels and rogues. And then there were the destitute ladies who'd rather try their hand at cards than be any man's mistress. "But I have no interest in bedding other women if that's what concerns you."

She shook her head. "No, I've already said I trust you. But I would like to come with you if I may."

Was she intent on courting scandal?

"I refuse to take my wife to a gaming hell."

"Why ever not? Besides, have you not made a terrible miscalculation?" When he raised a brow by way of a challenge, she added, "Someone must partner you when you play whist. What is the point of reading the signs when your partner lacks the necessary skill and could lose the game?"

She had a fair point though he'd thought of asking Tristan to accompany him. "And you want to be my partner? But you don't know how to play."

An impish grin revealed a certain smugness. "The other night, when you tried to teach me the rules, I feigned ignorance so you would spend time with me. I can play whist. Coupled with the ability to memorise the cards, I can be a formidable opponent."

"What, you expect me to believe you can remember the order of play?"

She folded her arms across her chest, the action pushing her breasts together. Damn, he'd almost forgotten how much he wanted to bed her. "There is only one sure way to prove my point. Put me to the test."

With his curiosity aroused, he took all the played cards from the table. "Then it shouldn't be too difficult to recall the order of these cards."

She inclined her head. "I had the ten of hearts, the four and three of clubs. The first card you turned over was the nine of diamonds, followed by the nine of hearts and then you drew the five of spades. Shall I continue?"

Bloody hell! If she could remember a whole pack, she'd prove to be invaluable.

"There's no need. We can play later this evening, and I shall put your skill to the test."

"Does that mean you'll take me with you?"

"You do realise people will slander your good name if they discover you frequent the seamier places."

"I am quickly becoming a lady who doesn't give a fig for what others say." She picked up a French bean and bit it in half. "Besides, as a lady who allows people to fornicate in her home, what more can they say?"

Guilt flared. "When I've made enough money, you won't have to share your home with anyone."

"Well, perhaps with some help, you might win enough from the sharps to rent a studio."

In moments of fanciful musings, he often dreamed of such a thing. "If I agree to take you, it will be only this once."

What harm would it do? If anything it would prove to the gossips that he loved his wife and craved her company.

"Of course. I would not wish to make a habit of socialising with immoral men. But I could read your notes and observe the sharps' behaviour, too."

He glanced at the clock on the mantel. "I might need persuading."

"Really? Then let's draw cards. If I win, you have no choice but to take me."

"You're my wife. I intend to take you in every way possible."

A chuckle burst from her lips. "Does your mind only follow one train of thought?"

"When it comes to you, yes." Despite the stays, her breasts wobbled as she laughed. He dabbed the corner of his mouth with his napkin to stop the excessive salivating. "May I remind you that sitting in your undergarments is hardly the way to test a man's resolve."

"Then the time for honesty is nigh. Tonight, I shall leave the connecting door open. A bed will be far more comfortable than the drawing room floor."

"But not nearly as much fun."

"Take me to the gaming hell, and I'll find a way to compensate you before we return home."

Intrigued by her proposal, Matthew dragged his hand down his face to temper his raging blood. "Agreed. Now shall we declare the winner of this bout?"

"Oh, I think it's fair to say we have both won this game."

CHAPTER 13

The Diamond Club, a notorious gaming hell that catered to the elite of society, stood nestled in the corner of the courtyard known as Pickering Place. Once a prime location for men to duel with pistols, due to its secluded position away from the main thoroughfare, it was not uncommon to find a gentleman slumped against the wall ready to end his own life.

Fortunes were made and lost at the exclusive club.

With a firm grip of Priscilla's hand, Matthew came to a stop outside the imposing black door with a lion-head knocker. He reached into his waistcoat pocket and removed a crisp calling card. "This club keeps a register of those who enter. They take my card and return it when I leave."

Priscilla wrapped the silk cloak across her chest and clutched his arm. "What if a gentleman forgets to bring a card?"

"Then someone inside must vouch for him. Failure to do so results in the manager politely asking him to leave. If one creates a fuss, his assistants are far from polite. Of course, things are different if you're a lady. Then you're given tokens to enter whenever you wish."

"Then I presume ladies are part of the entertainment," she mocked.

"Gentlemen come here to escape the pressures of daily life. Recklessness can be addictive. The club would be bankrupt if they didn't cater to their guests' every need."

While she'd appeared confident earlier, the slight tremble of her body and the lines marring her forehead conveyed a sudden apprehension.

"What will they make of me?"

"You're here with your husband. People will assume a scoundrel is educating an innocent in the ways of the world. No doubt I will be considered lucky to have a wife willing to break with convention. You will be considered an original, and consequently, can do no wrong."

"The only reason I'm here is to support you." She hugged his arm. "Though I suppose I should try to enjoy the experience."

"We are here to work," he reminded her. "I'm assured Lord Boden is playing tonight. Have you remembered the signs you must watch out for?"

For an hour after dinner and during the carriage ride to Pickering Place, Matthew had educated Priscilla in the language of the sharps. It was vital she understood every nuance: every subtle difference in movement or expression. To interpret the silent communication required concentration, a heightened awareness.

"A left eye twitch means he's playing a knave. Fingers clasped tightly together means it's a king," Priscilla recited. "It makes sense when you think of it. A knave is mischievous, a bit of a scamp. The eye twitch is to mimic a wink. The king is regal, and holds his fingers clasped to convey authority, and as a barrier against an attack."

To say her insight impressed him was an understatement. "You've just proved your point, Priscilla."

"What point?"

"That I need you." He paused, his words rousing an odd

feeling in his chest that he fought to suppress. "Not once has it occurred to me that there might be a logical definition for each movement."

"No doubt it made it easier for the sharps to learn the language."

"And easier for us to read the signs," he added, raising the brass knocker on the door and letting it fall. "Come, let us go inside and take refreshment. The hard play doesn't begin for a half hour. We've time to wander before we observe the rogues at work."

The stick-thin gentleman who opened the door and escorted them into the hall snatched the calling card from Matthew's hand as a starving man would a ten-pound note. Lifting his monocle, he studied the script before placing the card in a wooden box on the shelf behind him. The man turned and inclined his head. "Welcome, Mr Chandler." He opened the ledger on the desk before him, dipped his pen in the inkwell and made a few scrawls on the page. "I see you have brought a guest this evening. Is the lady to play at the tables?"

"Mrs Chandler is only here as an observer."

"Mrs Chandler? I see." From the dubious look gracing the man's weathered face, he assumed the woman parading as his wife was, in fact, his mistress. "You're aware I will need to enter her name in the guest book?"

"I am aware, yes."

"Will the lady require tokens to return unaccompanied?"

Priscilla spoke up. "I shall only ever attend with my husband."

The man dropped his monocle, the eyeglass dangling on a string tied around his neck, and looked down his beaky nose. "Then may I ask will you require the use of any other house services?"

Priscilla nudged Matthew's arm. He turned and whispered, "By services, he is asking if we require the use of a private room." Noting her frown, he added, "Do we desire the use of a bedchamber?"

Recognition finally dawned.

"Certainly not." Priscilla's blunt reply made the gentleman draw back. "As his wife, I have no need to take advantage of your hospitality," she continued a little more calmly.

An ache of disappointment filled Matthew's chest. The desperate need to bed his wife meant he was in a constant state of arousal. Even so, he'd not take her in a room used by every debauched sot, and there was but an hour or two to wait for the opportunity to sample her heavenly delights.

"Supper is served at midnight in the dining room. Should you need anything else you need only ask." The man held his open hand awkwardly in front of his chest only pulling it back when Matthew graced his palm with two sovereigns. "I wish you both a pleasant evening."

"What a strange fellow," Priscilla said as they followed the boisterous racket to the large drawing room situated at the back of the house.

"Don't let his frail demeanour fool you. He has the strength to slice a man's throat if the mood takes him."

"I can believe that. The man has the black beady eyes of a hawk ready to swoop on its prey." She glanced over her shoulder. "What shall I do with my cloak?"

"I suggest you keep it on. The ladies who frequent this establishment lack the morals you find in the ballroom and would think nothing of pilfering a reticule or silk cape. Now, hold on to me. Do not leave my side under any circumstances."

Firm fingers grasped the muscle in his upper arm. "What if we're separated in the crush? Should we agree on a meeting place? Should I wait in the hall?"

"Hell, no. As with any other house, the stairs lead to the bedchambers. If we're separated, then remain in the drawing room and wait by the window."

The thought of losing her amongst this rowdy rabble caused his heart to pound. Faint beads of perspiration formed on his brow as the need to protect her grew fierce. Having a wife had awakened newfound emotions he'd never encountered before. Then again, he'd never accepted responsibility for another person's welfare.

Her hand slid from his elbow down the length of his arm. Warm fingers entwined with his. "Then it's probably best we hold hands," she said. With their palms pressed together tight, he could feel the faint beat of a pulse. "The connection cannot easily be broken."

"Holding hands is an intimate gesture conducted in privacy," he teased as they hovered outside the drawing room door. "It's unheard of for a lady to display such a level of affection in public."

"But are we not in love? Are we not considered foolish and reckless in our habits?"

"We are."

"Then it's best not to disappoint the gossips," she said as they stepped into the room.

Swirls of smoke wafted through the air, the ghostly mist thick in places, transparent in others. The smell of tobacco clung to the coat of every gentleman they squeezed past. Fifty men, maybe more, were squashed into the small space. Some sat around the two tables positioned beneath the cut-glass chandeliers. Another group were arguing about the previous week's horse race at Leominster. Numerous ladies prowled around the perimeter, hunting for the latest gentleman willing to pay their rent.

Matthew responded to the nods and muttered greetings, all the while aware of Priscilla's hand pressed firmly against his. As expected, their attendance drew more than a few surprised glances.

"You seem to know a lot of people in here," Priscilla said as he drew her to an alcove away from the gaming tables. "Other than Lord Amberley, I have never seen any of these people before."

"One does not host scandalous parties without learning the names of every dissolute rake. The people who come here are not found sipping ratafia while discussing the merits of ribbons and lace."

"What? Do you think one cannot speak licentiously about sewing?" A sweet chuckle left her lips. "Does tugging on ribbons not excite you?"

"I suppose it depends on the context." Eager to hear more, he said, "I doubt even the most skilled courtesan could make ribbons sound remotely enticing."

"Is that a challenge? Or shall we have a wager?"

"Another wager? You know how to tempt me, Priscilla." Their palms grew hot as they continued to hold hands. "Prove me wrong, and I'll grant you anything your heart desires."

"Anything?"

"Anything."

"Will you answer another one of my probing questions on the way home?"

"Oh, I think I can do a little more than that."

"Very well." Straightening, she inhaled deeply, exhaled slowly. "As a woman who likes sewing, I find ribbon has many uses. Tied like a belt beneath my bodice it helps to keep my breasts pert. It makes them appear full, soft and round." As the words slipped seductively from her lips, his cock twitched in response. "The rich texture of velvet ribbon when worn against the skin always sends delicious tingles through my body. A strand of silk ribbon worn tight against the throat—"

"Enough." One more word and he was liable to burst out of his breeches. "You were right. When you speak, I find ribbon a thoroughly captivating topic. Now, perhaps we might continue this conversation in—"

"Chandler." A gruff, masculine voice called his name. "Chandler."

Matthew scoured the sea of heads to see Mullworth pushing his way through the crowd.

"Damn. One of my regular members is here." Mullworth was a debauched fool who spoke before engaging his brain. "He enjoys sharing stories of his conquests, likes to remind others of their licentious habits. I apologise if he says anything untoward."

Priscilla squeezed his hand. "Do your members know you're a fraud?"

"A fraud?"

"There is not a dishonourable bone in your body. You may play the role of libertine, but that is not the man I have come to know."

While he appreciated her faith in his character, he was a man who'd had many casual relationships with women. "Priscilla, whatever you think of me now bears no reflection on the things I've done in the past. No doubt Mullworth will take pleasure in taunting me."

"Is that another reason you keep me locked in my bedchamber during parties? Do you fear I'll not like what they say about you?"

For a reason unbeknown he wanted her to think he was worth more than the sum of his conquests. "I have no issue with the truth. It is the fabricated remarks of a wastrel I take umbrage with. Besides, the three of us conversing together is not good for business."

"Why?" Priscilla scoffed. "It is not considered *de rigueur* to speak with a married woman in the presence of her husband?"

"It has nothing to do with that. If Mullworth says one disrespectful word to you, I'm liable to knock his teeth down his throat."

"Chandler." The pot-bellied gentleman burst upon them. "You never mentioned you were coming to the club tonight." With wide eyes, he turned to Priscilla. "And if I'm not mistaken, is this not the lovely lady who dazzled in red?"

Suppressing his irritation, Matthew made the necessary introductions.

"My husband tells me you're a member of his club. Do you attend his parties often?"

"Never miss one." Mullworth's ruddy cheeks wobbled as he shook his head. "Always top for entertainment, though I recall you experienced an hour of merriment yourself the other evening."

"Merriment?"

"The waltz, my dear. The waltz."

"Well, I could not pass an opportunity to dance with my husband."

"Dance?" Mullworth chortled. "It looked to be a little more than that. No doubt the entertainment continued long after we'd left. Chandler is known for his prowess in the bedchamber."

Matthew coughed into his fist. "Remember you're talking to my wife." Although his fists ached to punch the man, he would rather not make a scene.

"Of course." Mullworth smiled at Priscilla and inclined his head. "I'm merely teasing Chandler here. What I mean is it was obvious you share a deep affection. Rest assured, he has not looked at another woman since you wed."

"Why would he?" Priscilla raised her chin. "Is it not my job to make certain he has no need to wander?"

"Too right. Too right." Mullworth put a hand on his stomach and chuckled again. His ravenous gaze travelled over every inch of Priscilla's body. "We all knew it would take an exceptional lady to capture Chandler's heart. Perhaps we might see you again when he holds the next party. A host needs a good hostess by his side, and to be guaranteed the company of such a ravishing creature will surely draw more members."

"I doubt I shall have cause to attend another party." Priscilla showed no sign that she found the man irritating nor did she fall for his flattery. "As I've already said, my only reason for attending was to dance with my husband."

"If dancing is what you love, I'm sure you'll find plenty of gentlemen willing to fill your card." Mullworth's slippery tone roused Matthew's ire. Knowing the man as he did, the last comment was an innuendo for a more sinful activity.

"Have a care, Mullworth. I'll not remind you again."

"You mistake me, sir," Priscilla said with a regal air. "It is my husband I love, not dancing. He will be the only man ever to claim a place on my card."

The words sounded so sincere Matthew almost believed they were true. Rather than scare the hell out of him, he found her declaration oddly reassuring. Mullworth gaped. There'd been no need to thump the man. Priscilla had knocked the wind out of him with one simple comment.

"Then Chandler here is a lucky fellow." Mullworth slapped him on the upper arm. "A lucky fellow, indeed."

A flurry of activity behind meant only one thing. The game was about to begin. They would need an optimum view if they had any hope of observing the language of cheaters.

"If you'll excuse us, Mullworth. I've brought my wife to witness the play at the tables." He clasped Priscilla's hand firmly. "No doubt I shall see you at my next gathering."

"Of course." Mullworth nodded. "The Devil himself couldn't keep me away."

CHAPTER 14

*H*ad Priscilla closed her eyes she would have known the moment the players entered the room. The hot, smoky air thrummed with nervous tension. Slow, baritone hums of conversation increased in speed and pitch. Excitement grew progressively louder as each man fought for the right to be heard.

Matthew pulled her through the crowd, squeezing her hand so tight her fingers were numb, no doubt a deathly shade of blue.

While The Diamond Club was a place for degenerates, most gentlemen stepped aside to allow her to pass, years of aristocratic breeding prevailing over the recently learnt manners of a rake.

In the crush, Matthew failed to infiltrate the first row of spectators gathered around the large rectangular table, and they had to make do with standing in the second row.

"It's not only the men at the table who gamble on the outcome of this game," Matthew whispered. The throng had quietened while waiting for the players to make their way to their seats. "Most of those in front of us have placed a wager, too."

Priscilla scanned the row of eager faces opposite. For some, the wide eyes and toothy grins would diminish with the outcome of each hand. "I wonder if their wives know they're gambling away the family fortune?" The slight bitterness in her tone revealed her own frustration at Uncle Henry's duplicity.

Matthew shuffled closer until his arm brushed against hers. "Those who gamble at this level are renowned for living a hedonistic lifestyle, openly boast about their wins and losses. Those men who are secretive about their pursuits are the ones who cause devastation for their family."

The words carried a hint of disdain. Of course, he hated lies. Deceitfulness was a trait she despised, too.

"Like my uncle you mean." An odd puffing sound left her lips. Uncle Henry enjoyed risking everything he owned on the turn of the cards or the roll of the dice. "I've spent years thinking his stingy habits stemmed from a need to protect his family. Now I know he needed every spare penny to keep the wolves from the door."

Matthew turned to face her fully. "I know your uncle has disappointed you. I understand what it's like to have everything you believed to be true ripped from you in one enlightening moment."

One did not need to have mystical powers to know he spoke of the secret pain that had hardened his heart. On the way home, she would use the time alone in the carriage to delve deeper. She had promised to compensate him for bringing her to the gaming hell, to offer the physical affection he craved. She hungered for his touch, too—not because it meant losing herself in the dizzy heights of pleasure but because the intimacy of the moment brought her ever closer to him.

A boisterous cheer disturbed her reverie.

"The players are about to take their seats," Matthew said. "Let us pray my information is correct and the sharps are playing tonight."

The lively throng parted to make way for the approaching players. Craning her neck, she caught the first glimpse of the four gentlemen as they sauntered to their seats at the card table.

Various members of the crowd stepped forward to give their favourite a slap on the back, tried not to stumble into them as they offered a slurred wish of luck or encouragement.

Priscilla cast Matthew a sidelong glance. His dark gaze lingered on the man with wiry red hair, bushy side whiskers and a bulbous nose.

"Well?" she asked, leaning closer. "Are we in luck?"

"The one with the flame-coloured hair is Mr Parker-Brown. The gentleman taking the seat opposite is his partner in whist, Lord Boden."

With a jutting chin, puffed chest and a look that radiated superiority, it was obvious no one thought more highly of Lord Boden than he did himself. His rigid posture and probing stare were enough to deter anyone from challenging his opinion.

"Boden looks as though he hates to lose," she said.

"The fellow has expensive tastes and looks for any way to fund his habits. He owns the fastest racehorse, the most extravagant phaeton. The gossips say he keeps three mistresses though there are always ladies vying for his attention."

Priscilla considered the gentleman's pretentious demeanour. His pale blue eyes were as cold and as desolate as the sea in Brighton on a winter's morning. There was nothing remotely handsome about his countenance, but then money was considered the most attractive quality by many.

"Pompous lords do nothing for me. I fail to see the appeal."

"I'm glad to hear it. May I remind you no one but me will ever claim a place on your dance card." The mischievous glint in his eyes held a wealth of promise though the fingers grazing over her hip sent irritating prickles up her side and across her shoulders.

Disgust made her stomach flip when she realised it couldn't be her husband's hand. She glanced over her shoulder to see Mr Mullworth hovering behind.

"Excuse me, my dear, I was trying to push to the front."

Not wanting to cause a scene, Priscilla offered a weak smile. "I fear it is rather a crush in here tonight. Everyone is keen to witness the game." Inclining her head to the leech, she turned to Matthew. "Can I stand in front of you?"

A frown marred her husband's brow as he scanned her face. "Why? What's wrong?"

"Mr Mullworth wishes to have a better view of the card game"—she lowered her voice—"and a crowd provides an ideal opportunity for a fellow with wandering hands to partake in a little exploration."

Matthew's penetrating stare shot to a point over her shoulder. The muscles in his jaw firmed and twitched as his nostrils flared. "If that degenerate touches you again, he'll lose more than the use of his blasted fingers."

"Pay it no heed." She placed a calming hand on his chest. The wild thump of his heart beating against her palm stirred hope in her breast. The need to protect surely stemmed from more than a sense of ownership. "The game is about to begin, and we need to keep our wits if we are to achieve what we came here to do."

With some reluctance, he dragged his gaze away from the goings-on behind. "As always you are a fountain of wisdom."

It was odd how one word could conjure a host of vivid images, stir one's sensibilities. Had Tristan's mother not lured the matrons into Lord Holbrook's garden on the pretence of seeing his splendid fountain, Priscilla would never have met Matthew Chandler. A sudden ache in her chest forced her to catch her breath.

Misinterpreting the sound of her anxiety, Matthew moved to stand behind. Measuring a good six inches taller, he pressed his body against hers, enveloping her in a warm embrace. Every fibre of her being responded instantly. The faint thrum of desire still lingered from their earlier flirtation in the drawing room. With each passing hour, with each new day, the craving to be near him grew.

"Is that better?" His mouth hovered but an inch from her ear. "Do you feel safer now?"

"I always feel safe with you." It was the most honest thing she'd ever said.

Matthew chuckled. "No one has ever spoken those words to me before. I'm regarded as one of the most dangerous men in the *ton*. Ladies of quality are taught to be afraid when in my presence. Perhaps I am losing my touch."

Priscilla leant back into him. "Well, I've recently discovered that I thrive on adventure. Dangerous men excite me."

"Men?" The single word brimmed with reproof.

"A slight slip of the tongue. What I meant to say was *you* excite me."

He bowed his head until the faint bristles on his jaw grazed her cheek. "The feeling is mutual."

No doubt anyone glancing their way would find her wide, satisfied grin odd considering she was staring at Lord Boden as he inspected the cards. "Hush now," she said though wished they had no reason to remain at The Diamond Club. "If we're not careful, we'll miss the first hand of whist."

A man wearing a forest-green tailcoat and burgundy waistcoat shuffled the deck. His nimble hands worked so quickly it made Priscilla dizzy just watching.

"The Diamond Club insist on using their own dealers," Matthew informed her. "There's no person alive who can keep up with Stanley's shuffling skills. A club's reputation rests on its ability to guarantee honest play. Anyone caught cheating is liable to face the barrel of a pistol at dawn."

"Then a man would have to be supremely confident to deceive the house." Priscilla noted Lord Boden's excessive preening: a flippant brush of the hair, a straightening of the sleeve. Either he found his fingernails fascinating, or he had a severe form of arthritis that caused his digits to curl into claws.

"One would need the cunning of the Devil."

"Then we should place our faith in divine intervention," Priscilla said as Stanley whipped the cards around the table, distributing the deck between all four players. The dealer placed the last card dealt face up.

"Spades are trumps," Matthew confirmed.

For the next few minutes, they focused all their efforts on watching the minute signals passing between Boden and Parker-Brown as each trick was played. The movements were so slight, practically impossible to read by the untrained eye.

"Watch when Boden takes a breath," Matthew muttered in her ear. "He gives the impression he's thinking, but each second equates to a number. Five seconds for a five and so on."

Priscilla watched the players with interest. "The sigh indicates the end of the breath."

As Matthew predicted during their earlier discussion, Boden's opponents won the first three hands, the last one by nine tricks to four. What better way to encourage a higher stake than to give one's challengers a false sense of security?

Boden won the next three hands to even the odds.

Mr Parker-Brown's arched brow suggested he was to play a queen next. Consequently, Lord Boden played his lowest card though they still won the trick. The sharps' winning streak continued for a few more rounds but then their luck took an unexpected turn for the worse.

Matthew bent his head, brushed his lips across her jaw merely to whisper privately. "They're deliberately losing. It will be a ploy to lure the weak-minded to try their luck. Lose tonight. Win tomorrow."

"It would make sense," she said, trying to focus on the conversation, though every time his mouth touched her ear desire shot through her like a lightning bolt. "Men are unlikely to gamble when the odds are stacked against them."

"I suspect that is …"

Priscilla missed the latter part of his comment. A sudden

prickle of awareness crept over her shoulders. She scanned the room, her gaze locking with another lady on the opposite side of the table. From her fiery red hair and arrogant curl of the lip, Priscilla knew the woman to be Lucinda Pearce. The lady placed her hand on the shoulder of a gentleman at her side, whispered something and laughed, though her penetrating stare conveyed nothing but disdain.

Anger bubbled away in Priscilla's belly. An absurd need to prove Matthew lusted after no one but her took hold. She leant back into her husband's warm body, her feet a little unsteady as the strange flurry of emotions caused spots of light to form in her vision.

Matthew placed firm hands on her shoulders. "Are you all right?"

"The smoky air is stifling." The lie only weakened her stance. "Miss Pearce is staring at me," she added truthfully. Honesty was the foundation of their union after all. "I would be lying if I said I did not find her intimidating."

"Then may I suggest you offer a confident smile." Nothing about his tone made her feel foolish. "Whenever my lips brush against your ear, close your eyes as though savouring my whispered endearments."

"I'm not very good at pretending."

"Who said anything about pretending?" His hands left her shoulders and settled on her hips. "Have I told you I cannot wait to taste your skin? That I long to rain kisses along the line of your collarbone, to devote my attention to satisfying your every need."

Liquid fire pooled between her legs. All the bones in her body felt limp. The constant chatter, the cheers and applause for the players, were drowned out by the sound of her heartbeat thumping in her ears.

"Have I told you how I long to be inside you, buried deep?" His hot breath breezed across her neck. Amidst the crowd of people, he pressed into her, the hard evidence of his arousal brushing against her buttocks. "Can you not feel the truth of it?"

Her legs almost buckled. "Take me home, Matthew." They were already courting gossip with their overfamiliar display.

"Do my words excite you, Priscilla? Am I not the dangerous man you long for?"

"You're everything I've ever longed for." The truth slipped from her lips without thought or censure.

After a brief pause, he said, "Come. We have seen enough here. Let us go home and see what delights the night shall bring."

Priscilla blinked and shook her head to force her mind back to reality. The shocked gasps of the spectators drew her attention. Judging by the smiles on Lord Boden's opponents faces, it was fair to assume the card sharps had lost. In light of the unexpected turn of events, numerous gentlemen approached the losers with an offer to play again.

"The game's over rather quickly." Priscilla suspected Lord Boden's solemn expression was merely a mask to hide his delight. "Whenever I've played whist it seems to go on for hours."

Lost in a dreamlike state as he stared at Mr Parker-Brown, it was a few seconds before Matthew spoke. "Here the games are short. Gentlemen are easily bored, quick to complain. The house takes a percentage of all winnings, and so the more games played, the more profitable the club."

"Stone the crows for all they're worth." Mullworth came to stand at their side, his ruddy cheeks and sickly sweet breath evidence of an excessive consumption of alcohol. "I bet thirty pounds Boden would win tonight. The blighter. I should have known his winning streak wouldn't last forever." Mullworth shook his head. "If only I'd known he'd lost at Hendrys this afternoon I might have held on to my wager."

Matthew cleared his throat. "You're saying this is the second time Boden has lost today?"

Mullworth's jowls wobbled as he nodded. "Lost a thousand to

Mr Marlow. Perhaps you should approach Boden and arrange another game. Might give you a chance to reclaim what you lost to him at the Holbrooks." The gentleman turned to Priscilla and gave a sly smile. "I'll keep this lovely lady company."

While Priscilla tried to convey a look of alarm without making it obvious, the man of the hour, Lord Boden, decided an introduction was due.

The arrogant lord stared at Mr Mullworth. "Good night, Mullworth. Best be on your way. There's a good fellow."

Mullworth's cheeks ballooned as though a thousand curses were trying to force their way out of his pursed lips. "Well … I … good night." With his head hung low, he scuttled off through the crowd.

A low chuckle rumbled at the back of Boden's throat.

Had it not been for her husband's plan to regain his losses from the prig standing before them, Priscilla would have thrust her nose in the air and called the man to task for his lofty manners.

Offering a satisfied sigh, the lord turned to Matthew. "Ah, Chandler. I've not heard from you of late. I was expecting a visit to repay your vowel though I hear you've been somewhat occupied." Stony-faced, the man's lips twitched as he inclined his head to Priscilla. "Mrs Chandler. While most would express pleasure upon hearing of your recent nuptials, I fear no lady of quality wants to visit her husband in debtors' prison."

Priscilla cleared her throat. "Then I must assume that no lady of quality has ever been in love, my lord. As you are now aware, money is as easily lost as won. Loyalty, once earned, is constant."

Boden arched a brow. "Such strength of character is commendable, my dear. I wonder if you will feel the same when you're forced to bid farewell to your maid. Will you still hold your husband in high regard when your clothes are threadbare, and he has drunk himself into oblivion?"

The muscles in Matthew's cheek twitched. "You underestimate me on many levels. A man with nothing left to lose makes for a formidable opponent. But rest assured, you shall have your money in the next few days."

Priscilla did not hold out much hope of that being the case. Her parents had died penniless. Any dowry offered was provided for by her uncle Henry's estate, but the man had made no motion to settle. The proportion he'd stipulated as part of her inheritance was probably worthless given his current financial situation.

"You're far too reckless to pose a threat." Boden's tone conveyed his contempt. "I trust you will honour your word. Any stain on your character will inevitably affect your wife. Then again, perhaps you lack her faith in love and loyalty." Boden sneered. "Of course, I am always open to a wager."

"A wager?" Matthew's narrowed gaze suggested confusion, but Priscilla knew he had been waiting for an opportunity to challenge the lord. Surely what Matthew knew of the sharps' game play was enough to push the odds in his favour.

Boden examined his fingernails with an air of indifference. "A rematch. Double or quits. You win, I wipe your debt. You lose, you owe me twenty thousand."

"And why would I do that?" Matthew countered. "I have the funds to pay."

"Because you know I'm on a losing streak and you're a gentleman who scoffs at the idea of defeat. Tell me honestly, do you not find the thought of wiping the smug grin off my face appealing?"

"Punching the smug grin from your face would be my preference."

It would take more than a threat to weaken the lord's self-assured stance. "Unless you wish to stand back-to-back at dawn, I'm afraid cards must be the combat of choice."

Matthew pursed his lips to give the impression he was deep in thought, but Priscilla knew he was merely stringing the lord along. "Will we have random partners?"

Boden's mouth curled up into a conceited smirk. "I will choose my own partner. I'll not play with a dimwit."

"Then name your man."

"Parker-Brown will partner me. We work well together. There is no one I trust more."

The revelation was far from shocking.

"Then it is only fair I name my partner," Matthew said.

"Of course." Boden gave an indolent wave. "Name your man."

"Man?" A chuckle burst from Matthew's lips. "I name Mrs Chandler as my partner. We work well together. There is no one I trust more."

For the first time since setting eyes on the pompous lord, his passive expression appeared ruffled. "Choose someone else. I'll not take money from a woman."

"When you take money from my husband are you not also taking it from me?" As a woman's possessions became the property of her husband upon marriage, Boden could offer no argument. "Whether I play or not, for me the outcome is the same. You can have no other objection. Unless you find my presence intimidating."

Boden stroked his chin as he considered her. "Men play ruthlessly, Mrs Chandler. I'll not hold my tongue or bide my manners under any circumstances. Feminine gasps and sighs put me off my game."

"You need not concern yourself with me, my lord." A few weeks ago she might have faltered under the lord's merciless stare. "One needs a strong constitution when one's home is a venue for scandalous parties. I have seen and heard enough to eradicate all delicate sensibilities."

"You'll find my wife is a true original," Matthew added. "There is not much that fazes her. But if you refuse to accept her as my partner, I'll not play."

Matthew stepped forward and placed his hand on Priscilla's lower back. "Come. Let us be on our way."

"Do not be so hasty, Mr Chandler. Will you not give a fellow a chance to reply?" There was a faint hint of desperation in Boden's voice which he tried to mask. "I have made my decision and agree to your terms. Mrs Chandler may partner you in the game. After all, what gentleman would reject an opportunity to sit next to such a fascinating creature?"

Creature? Was she supposed to find the comment flattering? The odious lord thought himself far superior.

"Then might I suggest you come to Grosvenor Street on Friday evening? I'm hosting a party, and our wager will provide amusement for my guests."

"Are you sure you want an audience when I take you for twenty thousand pounds?"

Matthew opened his mouth but snapped it shut. He offered the lord a bow though the gesture failed to convey respect. "Only a fool would attempt to predict the hand of Fate."

With a firm hand, Matthew guided Priscilla away.

"Chandler," Boden called out after him. "May I commend you on making at least one wise decision."

"What?" Matthew glanced back over his shoulder. "You think a man is wise to risk a fortune?"

Priscilla felt Boden's penetrating gaze like an icy chill breezing across her skin.

"I was not referring to the game, Chandler, but to your wife. It appears there are some treasures money cannot buy."

CHAPTER 15

*a*s any gentleman with a hardened heart knew, jealousy was a foreign emotion. Mental unease served no purpose. To experience the debilitating condition, one must fear their rival, lack faith in their own abilities, or care so deeply for something all rational thought was lost to them.

Matthew ushered Priscilla into their carriage, pretending that the twisting knots in his belly stemmed from his anger towards Lord Boden and his cheating accomplices. The tight pain in his chest he attributed to inhaling the smoky air at The Diamond Club.

"You should have a care around the likes of Boden," he said as they settled into opposite seats. There was a hard edge to his tone that he couldn't suppress. His sour mood was reflected in the way he yanked down the blinds. "The man covets anything unusual and rare. From the look he gave you, I expect he will look for an opportunity to further your acquaintance."

"But he knows we're married." A frown marred her brow. No doubt her pure heart struggled to accept Boden's assumption that she would be unfaithful. "Why would he waste his time?"

"Based on my reputation, he will presume we share a relaxed

attitude to matrimony." Damn. In taking her to a gaming hell, coupled with her comments about the scandalous antics at his parties, Boden would think Priscilla game for more than amorous flirtation. "He will attempt to seduce you."

A snigger burst from her lips. "You make me sound like the catch of the Season. Or a famed actress with the ability to rouse a man to sin with nothing more than a pout."

It was no laughing matter. Some men did not seek permission but merely took what they wanted. "Don't underestimate the lure of a woman with a strong will. Men like Boden thrive on power."

"Oh, so you mean it is not my beguiling eyes or curvaceous figure that has him captivated?" Despite her apparent amusement, there was a thread of disappointment in her tone.

Matthew noted the same flash of inadequacy in her eyes that he'd witnessed that night in Lord Holbrook's garden. "I didn't say that. My excessive salivating is surely a testament to your physical attributes. But every man is searching for the one unique quality that speaks to his soul. Boden's happens to be competence."

She raised a curious brow, and he knew what question would follow. "And what of you, Matthew? What quality speaks to your soul?"

"I sold my soul to the Devil the moment I entertained his flock for money."

"You didn't sell it. You merely placed it elsewhere, locked away in an iron chest for safe keeping. But from what little I know of you I suspect honesty is the unique quality you seek."

"You're right." He knew what it felt like to be betrayed by those one loved the most, to be sacrificed for a lie. "The moment I doubt a person's motive is the moment I cast them out of my life."

Priscilla straightened and shuffled to the edge of the seat. "Do you trust me, Matthew? Do you believe all that I tell you?"

He wanted to say that he would never trust another soul ever again. But he trusted Tristan. He was still learning to trust

Uncle Herbert, hoped one day to feel the same way about Priscilla.

"I imagine trust takes many years to build." The lie left a bitter taste in his mouth which forced him to add, "Then again, it is often those you've known the longest that prove to be a disappointment."

She stared at him. A few drawn-out seconds passed before she spoke. "Then believe me when I tell you that whatever happens between us tonight, happens because I want it to. Not because I feel it is my duty as your wife, or because of some silly wager we made earlier. The desire to be close to you is overwhelming."

"Well, you promised to show me your gratitude for taking you to the gaming hell." He sounded like a cad, a man detached from reality who made light of any emotion as a way of avoiding the truth.

Without warning, she crossed the carriage and fell into the seat next to him. "Tonight I will give you all I have. I will give you myself wholeheartedly. Completely." A dainty hand came to rest on his thigh. "I will hold nothing back. You will feel the truth in my touch, taste it on my lips." Her fingers crept higher. "I am yours to take in any way you desire. But first, you must agree to give me something in return."

"Oh, I intend to give you everything I have and more."

"I'm pleased to hear it."

She stroked the evidence of his growing arousal. Remarkably, all other thoughts dissipated leaving nothing but the urge to bed her. With nimble fingers she unbuttoned the placket of his breeches, her warm hand slid down and curled around his cock. The slight tremble in her fingers enhanced his pleasure.

Bloody hell!

His minx of a wife massaged his manhood, her inexperience heightening his excitement. The realisation that she had never touched another man like this before made his heart swell just as much as his cock.

"I want to try something I witnessed in the garden," she said, still pumping his erection. "I want to show you that your happiness is important. But it demands that I trust you to be mindful of my lack of skill."

Lack of skill? The lady was doing remarkably well. Amidst the hazy fog of desire disturbing his mind and vision, he struggled to put a picture to her words.

"I've thought of nothing else all evening," she purred, "and in return, I want your trust."

The word caught him off guard, dampened his ardour, only somewhat. He blinked, attempted to form a question, but events took a sudden unexpected turn that left him speechless.

Priscilla pushed him back against the squab, held his cock in her hand and lowered her head. Past experience did little to prepare him, for his wife liked to tease, liked to rain kisses on the head, down the shaft, lick the tip to determine if she liked the taste. Soft lips settled over him, and he entered her moist mouth … Holy hell! The rush of pleasure forced his head back. He had married the goddess Venus in the guise of a vestal virgin.

Inexperience proved enticing. Perhaps fearing taking him fully into her mouth, she practised bobbing up and down, stopping a short way past the head. Seven shallow sucks were followed by a long, deeper one. Then six shallow, two long. A pleasurable hum resonated in her throat, the sound sending vibrations through his cock. At five shallow sucks, he knew she'd found a rhythm.

The mounting tension blew his mind. He wanted to grab her hair, thrust up into her wicked mouth but feared doing anything to ruin what was the most gratifying moment of his life. Instead, he clutched the seat, closed his eyes and let his wife do what she wanted.

Matthew was almost at the point of release when he realised Priscilla wouldn't know what to expect.

"That's enough, love," he panted. Dragging a handkerchief

from his pocket, he finished the job with his hand. The pure power accompanying his climax robbed him of breath though he was aware of the satisfied grin filling his face.

He looked up, his eyes locking with Priscilla's. The peachy-glow touching her cheeks, the full, swollen lips still parted as her own breath came quickly, was an entrancing sight to behold.

Something had happened to him in that lust-fuelled moment. A connection formed, one deeper than anything he'd ever known. Not because she had performed such a scandalous act in a carriage. But due to her utter lack of knowledge, it must have taken an immense amount of courage to give him what he wanted. It was a selfless act. An act to strengthen the bond between them. An act of trust.

"You did not have to do that," he panted, still trying to catch his breath.

"I know. Regardless of the fact you're my husband, everything I do is because I want to. Duty plays no part."

"I've heard many men say their wives find such an intimate act abhorrent. Did you find it so?"

She pondered the comment. "While it doesn't feel completely natural, there is something empowering about having you at my mercy, controlling your pleasure and rendering you helpless."

The vision of her tying him to the bed whilst she rode him to completion popped into his head. Damn. Could he think of nothing else but bedding his wife? "Does that mean you might enjoy seducing me again?"

A coy smile touched her lips. "I might."

The carriage jerked and rumbled to a halt. Matthew leant forward and raised the blind. "We're home." Now he could indulge his desires and do what he'd spent the last few nights avoiding.

Priscilla touched his arm. "Wait. Can we remain in the carriage for a moment?"

"Why? Do you have more delights in store for me? I should

warn you, a stationary carriage rocking and swaying in the street will give the gossips plenty to talk about."

"Don't excite yourself. I wanted to ask you something that's all."

The euphoria that accompanied his release still thrummed through his veins which was why he dismissed the footman waiting outside the door and readied himself for what he suspected would be a probing question. After all, he could hardly refuse such a simple request.

"What would you like to know, Priscilla?"

She swallowed visibly—the vision rousing an image of their passionate encounter mere moments before—and then straightened.

"Well, I suppose it's a question of two halves as I suspect there is a connection. Tell me, what did Tristan do for you that would see you marry a woman you cared nothing for?"

The question rebounded back and forth in his mind. It wasn't the question that rattled him, more the realisation that his feelings for Priscilla had changed since that first meeting.

"Before I answer, perhaps you might reveal the other half of your question."

She nodded. "Does the debt you owe to Tristan have something to do with the reason you're estranged from your family?" She paused while she scanned his face. "I deserve to know the truth, Matthew. I understand why you're so guarded, but tell me this, and I promise to ask nothing more from you."

A gaping hole opened in his belly. What if there came a time when she didn't need him? What if she no longer came to him with her questions and curiosities?

"To understand the situation, I must answer the second question first." To reveal the truth would mean revisiting the scene in the woods, acknowledging that money meant more to his family than honour and loyalty. "You want my trust, Priscilla. Then understand that, other than to Tristan, I have not spoken of this to anyone. As such, I am placing my faith in you. Listen but do not offer words of comfort, pity or wisdom. After this moment, I want to leave the past behind and never speak of it again."

"I understand."

She put her hand on his thigh. This time the gesture was meant to reassure him.

"Please." He took hold of her hand and placed it in her lap. "Do not get upset, but I would rather you sat in the seat opposite." Just being near her stirred emotions he did not understand. To be blinded by sentiment might make him look at his situation from a different perspective. It had taken years to come to terms with what had happened. He had neither the time nor the inclination to begin again.

"Of course." The croak in her voice belied her confident smile.

Damn. Later, when they were alone in bed, he would lavish her with attention. He would take his pleasure, too, hoping to eradicate the sombre mood that gripped him whenever he thought of his past.

He opened his mouth to speak but paused. Did he really want to relive those dark moments? Did she really need to know? But then he supposed he owed her an explanation.

"Have you ever had a premonition? Have you ever woke with the thought that the day held some significance though you knew not what?"

"No." Her word was as quiet as a whisper.

"I knew the moment I opened my eyes that I should hurry to the window. It was early. A blanket of mist clung to the ground. I watched my father stride across the lawn, heading towards the woods bordering our estate." To speak quickly prevented the images lingering in his mind. "The morning was cold, damp, and I noted he had no coat."

"You were at Moorlands, I assume."

He nodded.

"How old were you?"

"Ten."

"Just a boy, then."

He nodded again. "I don't know why but I had an urge to follow him. With no time to dress, I took a blanket off the bed and ran along the path. I found my father sitting on a log in a clearing. I froze, worried he might be angry that I'd left the house in my nightclothes." Matthew paused. To his own ears, his voice sounded childlike. His heart was racing. He could smell the earthy scent in the air, could feel the same paralysing sense of doubt, of fear. "I hesitated a moment too long. The gunshot rang through the air seconds before his body slumped forward and hit the ground."

Priscilla gasped and covered her mouth with her hand. There was a pained silence. "Oh, Matthew. How awful. The trauma of witnessing such a thing must never leave you."

"It doesn't. But that was only the beginning of a period of psychological torment."

Priscilla dabbed the corner of her eye with her finger. "What did you do?"

"I raced to the house to alert my mother. She sent me to my room and then, with the help of my brother who was fifteen at the time, set about creating the deception."

"Deception?"

"We were to tell the coroner it was an accident. That we were out hunting with Lord Watts from the neighbouring estate. My brother, Simon, said he'd witnessed Lord Watts shoot at a deer, that my father had strayed from his line. Simon adept at telling tales, but I was not. Despite my mother's distress, I couldn't do it. Perhaps my reluctance stemmed from anger, disappointment in my father. Pain. Confusion. I don't know. Why would he do such a cowardly thing? Why would he bring shame on his family?" Matthew shrugged. There was no point trying to analyse the thoughts of a desperate man.

"And so what happened?"

"Due to the nature of his close friendship with my mother, Lord Watts lied to the coroner." He chose not to add that the lord spent many nights thereafter in his mother's bed or that they were lovers for years until the fellow married a debutante twenty years his junior. "Simon lied, too, as did my mother's uncle. Several men came to inspect the body. They all supported the cause of death as accidental. After all, why would a man whose bloodline brimmed with honourable men take his own life? Why would a peer shoot his friend in front of witnesses?"

It wasn't the lie that hurt him, he understood that, but the disdain shown to a child who'd always been told to tell the truth.

"From then on they treated me differently. To rationalise what I'd seen I tried to talk to my mother, but she insisted I was just a silly boy who made up stories. When the nightmares woke me from sleep—no one came. When I … when I soiled my bed in those moments when fear still gripped me—no one came."

Priscilla cleared her throat. "Is that why you keep your family at a distance?"

"She sent me away to school, told the master I had a wild imagination which often led to endless lies." His tone was hard now, unyielding. "The nightmares continued, as did the other embarrassing aspect that accompanied my trauma. But I was no longer alone at night. This time I was beaten for it, ridiculed, made to feel worthless. That was until Tristan came. Until I stopped being a victim and fought back. Indeed, I didn't stop fighting until I'd bloodied every boy's nose who'd dared taunt me."

Silence ensued. The wild beat of his heart and the sharp crack of a gunshot were the only sounds echoing in his ears.

"And so that is why you insist on honesty." Priscilla's soft voice drifted through the carriage.

"Let me be clear. If you ever lie to me, we could not reside in the same house. We would be married in name only." Twenty years of bitterness was evident in his voice. "I would not tolerate your deception." In truth, it would kill him to discover he'd been wrong about her.

"Then I pray I always have the strength of character to be truthful." She glanced down at her hands resting in her lap. "But in telling people we are in love, we have lied, Matthew."

"Have we?"

"Do not try to offer one of your alternative explanations. A lie is a lie."

"I have not lied. Do we not share a passionate affection? Do we not take pleasure in each other's company?" He admired her, yearned to claim her body. It was the closest thing to love he'd ever known. "I am committed to no one but you."

She crinkled her nose. "Yet it is not the same as true love."

"Oh, and I suppose you have experience in that regard."

"Some. My father was a poet. My mother was happy to live frugally to allow him to pursue his life's work. They found beauty in each other, in nature. Never in wealth or title. They cared nothing for other people's lofty opinions, had nothing to prove." A long, drawn-out sigh left her lips. "To love someone is to accept them for who they are. To love someone is to nurture their soul as much as your own. While there are varying degrees of affection, there is only one love like my parents shared."

To him, such a love was inconceivable.

"I doubt that sort of love is possible for everyone. Perhaps time will prove otherwise." Her idea of love spoke of self-sacrifice, of surrendering oneself to another. It went beyond his capabilities. It was a step too far on a road he'd not intended to travel. "As I've said before, I live for the moment. A need to celebrate our undeniable attraction is the only thought currently plaguing my mind."

Priscilla smiled. "I think you use lustful activities to eradicate the pain of the past." With a shrug, she added, "It is just my honest opinion."

Matthew inclined his head. "Then I must respect it." To give any thought to the comment would only distract him from the only thing he wanted. "Perhaps we should go inside and test your theory."

As always a nervous energy filled the air whenever one mentioned indulging their desires.

Priscilla shuffled forward and touched his knee. "Then take me to bed, Matthew. Love me in the only way you know how."

CHAPTER 16

hey parted ways on the landing, each heading to their prospective bedchambers to wash and change into nightclothes. Priscilla glanced over her shoulder, noted Matthew's self-assured strides, the certainty in every movement.

So why were her hands shaking?

Why did it feel as though her heart and stomach had swapped places?

She had been intimate with him before. Heavens, she had just performed an act considered lewd by most matrons' standards. The advice to all newly married ladies was clear. Never deny one's husband his conjugal rights else he shall seek fulfilment elsewhere. Nevertheless, some activities he may ask a lady to perform are commonplace in brothels, not the marriage bed. Once one lowers one's standards, it's impossible to regain one's dignity.

Oh, well.

When one married a scoundrel, partaking in sinful deeds was inevitable.

Drawing in a deep breath, Priscilla entered her chamber.

Illuminated by the golden glow of the fire burning low in the grate and the two candle lamps positioned on the night tables, the scene spoke of seduction. The soothing ambience did little to settle her nerves. The dark shadows flickering on the wall seemed to perform a wild and erotic dance. Tonight, she would be at her husband's mercy. She would be a slave to his wicked fingers. The feel of his naked body, skin pressed against skin, would feed her growing addiction to him.

Lost in a vision of romantic whimsy, Priscilla tugged at the ribbons on her cloak. Marriage to a stranger should have been a cold, emotionless affair. Yet a host of feelings swirled around in her chest whenever she looked at her husband. Like a precious object on a high shelf, love was within her grasp. She could see it, almost touch it. All she needed to do was stand on tiptoes and reach higher, believe it was possible.

The light knock on the door disturbed her reverie.

Anne peered around the jamb. "I thought you might need my help." The maid crept into the room and closed the door.

The chime of midnight had passed, and so Priscilla wouldn't keep the maid too long. "Just loosen my stays, and I can do the rest."

"I'll help you undress." Determined to be of service, Anne stood behind Priscilla and unfastened the buttons on her dress. "The hour is late. No doubt you're eager to get to your bed."

Eager was an understatement.

For days she'd waited for Matthew to come to her room. But what if she proved to be a disappointment? Perhaps if she wore something to excite him, something to heat his blood, it might help. But what? She had nothing suitable. Nothing other than the clothes of her birth. The thought of him walking in to find her stretched naked on the bed caused a fluttering sensation in her belly.

Anne helped her out of her dress and undergarments and shook out the plain cotton nightgown with ruffled sleeves and buttons that fastened up to the throat.

"Wait." Priscilla raised her hand as Anne gathered the nightgown up ready to place it over Priscilla's head. "Are all my night-clothes as plain and simple?" Women like Lucinda Pearce probably wore diaphanous silk to bed.

Anne's lips drew thin. A look of pity flashed across her face. "There was no time to purchase anything new, and your uncle refused to accept you needed a trousseau."

It had nothing to do with acceptance. Uncle Henry lacked the funds to pay. Besides, he was a person who despised extravagance and saw it as her husband's duty to provide more than the basics.

"Then a cotton sack it is." With a sigh of resignation, Priscilla held her arms up and shrugged into the unflattering garment.

With pursed lips and a compassionate gaze, Anne stepped back. "Do you remember the time when your aunt brought you the pink kid gloves presented in that ugly box? The shop had run out of fine tissue and so had covered them in brown paper."

"Of course. They're the softest gloves I own." Priscilla hugged her hands to her chest. "I wish I had twenty pairs in an assortment of colours."

"The packaging did nothing to detract from their quality or beauty. If anything, I believe it made you cherish them all the more."

Discovering the gem buried inside the odd box had stolen her breath. "The disappointing packaging made them appear all the more spectacular."

"Precisely. I doubt cotton is any different. Of course, once a person is used to seeing presents wrapped in brown paper it doesn't hurt to throw in the odd piece of fancy tissue."

A chuckle burst from Priscilla's lips. "Then we must go shopping soon." A sudden rap on the dressing room door startled them. "Quick. You may leave me, Anne."

"But don't you want me to brush out your hair, madam?"

"No. There's no time." She'd spent too long daydreaming. Anne almost stumbled over her own feet as Priscilla ushered the maid out into the hall. "Besides, the unwrapping of presents builds anticipation."

Fearing Matthew might think the delay meant she had changed her mind, she closed the door and hurried to the dressing room. With trembling fingers, she brushed her hand down the cotton gown and then opened the connecting door.

"I thought you'd fallen asleep." Matthew's amused gaze travelled from her fancy coiffure down to her frumpy nightgown. "Do you need a little more time? Or is this intriguing contrast a means of piquing my interest?"

Priscilla patted her golden locks, remembered she was a diamond in a pond full of pebbles. "I thought you might like to remove the pins. I thought you might like to unravel the curls, thread your fingers through my hair."

He raised a sinful brow of approval. "What, as one would unwrap a present?"

"Yes, exactly like that."

One look at his loose shirt hanging over his breeches, and the dusting of dark hair evident through the open neck, she knew she'd be ripping the wrapping off *her* gift.

"Then you do intend to step aside and let me in."

Priscilla steeled herself, for her stomach was busy performing acrobatic flips. "I intend to grant you whatever your heart desires." She turned and sauntered into her chamber, could feel his stare sliding over her back like a lover's caress.

"I thought we could share a drink, play a few hands of cards." Matthew came into the room, placed a crystal decanter and glass on the dressing table. The ruby-red liquid glistened in the muted light—dark and rich, just like his voice. "Or we could talk if you prefer."

In accordance with the obvious plan to make her feel at ease, his voice was calm, controlled, that of a man skilled in bedroom repartee. She wanted to convey the same air of self-assurance.

She wanted him to see her as an alluring woman, not a child to be cared for and coddled.

"You want to drink, talk and play cards?" Feigning the grace of a duchess, she drifted over to him and placed her palm on his chest. "If this is part of your plan to seduce me, then I can save us both some time. I don't intend to offer an objection."

The tip of his tongue traced the seam of his lips. "Then I don't intend to wait a moment longer."

Curling a hand around her nape, Matthew pulled her closer. Startled, she gasped, and he covered her mouth with an urgent kiss, devoured her with a hunger so opposed to his previously cool demeanour. Like a man dying of thirst, he clasped her face with both hands and drank long and deep. Just his taste—a raw masculine essence she found highly addictive—sent her head spinning.

Currents of desire swept through her body as their tongues touched, tangled. The muscles in her core pulsed. A sense of longing gripped her, and she clutched his shoulders, his guttural groan filling her mouth as he strove to delve deeper.

God, there was nothing she needed more than him.

Impatient to touch his bare skin, Priscilla grasped his fine lawn shirt, yanked it up to slide her hands under, but the blasted thing was too long.

"Here, allow me," he said in a languid drawl as they broke for breath. "You're a little greedy tonight."

"Greedy!" She was ravenous. "Well, I have waited patiently for the best part of a week."

"And whose fault is that? I recall rattling the door until it almost came off its hinges."

"It wouldn't do to make things too easy for you. In fact, I think you should put on a show for me." She had to do something to even the odds, something to make the moment more memorable—to set it apart from all his other encounters.

"A show?" He brushed his lips tenderly against hers as he

147

spoke. "So you want me to perform, my lady. Shall I juggle with a pair of ripe, juicy apples or teach you to swallow a sword?"

Oh, he was exceptional at this game.

"I have had some experience swallowing swords. But I'd like to watch you undress."

Matthew jerked his head back, but his sly smile suggested he was more than game. "As the saying goes, one good turn deserves another. I'm more than happy to go first."

Excitement bubbled in her belly. "It will be interesting to see if the reality lives up to what I imagined." There was an arrogance to her tone that was so unlike her, but it served her purpose.

"Minx. Be sure to tell me if you like what you see." He took three steps back. Grabbing the hem of his shirt, he crossed his arms over his chest and pulled the garment over his head.

Priscilla covered her mouth with her hand for fear of drooling. He stood before her, blindingly handsome. Broad shoulders gave way to well-defined arms. Small, dark nipples peaked under the heat of her gaze. Her fingers tingled to touch the ebony hair gracing his muscular chest.

"Now the breeches," she said, though the lump in her throat made it almost impossible to breathe. Muscles she didn't even know she had clenched at the prospect of joining with him.

With his confident gaze locked on hers, he undid the buttons, pushed the breeches slowly down over his hips to reveal his erection. "As you can see, I am rather excited about the prospect of sharing your bed." His manhood was as solid and impressive as she'd witnessed in the confines of the carriage.

Priscilla's mouth felt dry. "Turn around."

"What, you're more curious to see my backside than my manhood?" His regal stance emphasised his powerful thighs and slim hips. Lord, she wanted to study every inch of him.

"I've surveyed that part of your anatomy from close quarters." And she would gladly do so again.

A mischievous smile formed on his lips. "Would you care to

carry out another examination? I would be more than willing to act as patient."

"Turn around." *Incorrigible* didn't even begin to define Matthew Chandler.

He bowed, held his hands up and turned to face the wall. "Feast your eyes, for soon it will be my turn."

Despite finding amusement in their game, her body ached to join with him. Indeed, she couldn't wait a moment longer. "Is there a part of your body that isn't muscular?"

"I'm afraid I'm a little out of shape. But an hour of vigorous exercise and I believe you'll be more than impressed with the results. Now, can—"

"Wait. Don't turn around yet," she said, the sound of her voice disguising the fact that she'd dragged her nightgown over her head. "Give me a few more seconds." She pulled the pins from her hair and shook out the curls. "I'd just like to touch you if I may."

"I'm all yours, love. You may do what you wish."

Lust banished all nerves. Naked, she stepped forward. Her breasts felt heavy, her erect nipples ached. Just walking teased the sensitive spot between her legs. She touched his buttocks, ran her hands up over his back.

"Your skin is softer than I imagined." Stepping up on tiptoes, she pressed her lips to his shoulder.

A pleasurable moan filled the air. "God, Priscilla, you know how to tease a man. Do you intend to torture me much longer?"

Suppressing a chuckle, she slid her arms around his waist, hugged him tight so that her breasts were squashed against his back. "I've longed to feel the warmth of your skin."

"Bloody hell. You're naked."

A wide grin formed. "I thought that was the idea."

CHAPTER 17

*W*ith a sudden sense of urgency, Matthew stepped out of Priscilla's embrace and swung around to face her.

Mere days ago he'd told himself one woman's body was the same as another. After observing the naked physique of many courtesans and mistresses, the female form no longer sent the blood rushing through his veins. *Indifferent* was perhaps the best word to describe his response.

So why did his cock throb at the sight of his wife's porcelain skin?

Why did one glance of her soft round breasts render him mute?

Damn, his blood was pumping so fast he struggled to stand. "As you've skipped the revealing, I believe it is my turn to touch." His hungry gaze travelled over her luscious body. Hell, it took all the strength he possessed not to ravage her senseless. "It's my turn to experience the warmth of your skin."

She held her arms out. "I'm yours, Matthew. You may do as you wish."

Although she'd repeated his phrase, the thought that she

belonged to him awakened a primitive need to claim, to protect. He placed both hands on her shoulders, let his fingers glide down her arms, drift across to graze over her breasts. The rosy peaks hardened instantly. He bent his head, unable to resist the urge to flick the tip with his tongue.

She sucked in a breath, threaded her fingers through his hair as he lavished both breasts with equal attention.

"I want to taste every inch of you, Priscilla." With his swift movements conveying his urgency, he scooped her up into his arms and laid her down on the edge of the bed. "And I do have a debt to repay."

When he knelt on the floor and draped her legs over his shoulders, she clutched the coverlet. "What are you doing?" The nervous hitch in her tone was evident.

"Fulfilling a fantasy and returning the favour." Raining chaste kisses along her inner thigh, he worked up to the sweet spot already swollen and crying out for relief.

One long, light lick dragged a moan from her lips.

Good. At least she'd not jumped off the bed in disgust. Indeed, when he increased the pressure and speed, her breathless pants confirmed he was doing something right. The side-to-side motion proved to be a favourite though she was taking longer to reach her peak than he'd expected.

There was no rush, he told himself, although he was about ready to burst. The best lovers were the selfless ones. And he would rather an honest reaction than one feigned purely to serve his ego.

"Oh, God." The two promising words left her lips as she bucked against his tongue. She was close. "Please, Matthew, I need you. I need you now."

Patience was a virtue neither of them possessed.

"Please, I beg you."

In his dreams, she begged to be fucked. Only this was nothing like he imagined. There was nothing base, nothing crude or vulgar about his need to bury himself inside her. It meant so much more than that. The pleasurable sensation as he surrendered to the will of their bodies and thrust into her core hit him somewhere deep in his chest.

She was so warm, so wet, so utterly divine.

He filled her full, withdrew slowly—repeated the exquisite motion again and again. The moist sound fuelled his desire.

An overwhelming sense of euphoria enveloped him, growing in intensity as the muscles in her core hugged him tighter with each delicious slide. The foreign feeling disturbed his rhythm, to the point he scarcely knew what was happening.

"Don't stop," she gasped, gripping him with cushioned thighs. She dug her fingers into his buttocks and forced him to move faster. Harder. Deeper.

Understanding her demand, he angled his hips to stimulate her better. Thank the lord his efforts had the desired effect. A few rapid movements left her panting and writhing beneath him, clawing at his back, begging for more.

Bloody hell!

He'd be lucky to last another minute. They continued to rock in exquisite harmony until she cried out.

"*Matthew!*" His name had never sounded so good. "Oh, God."

The need to join her in ecstasy drove him harder. The final stroke dragged a guttural groan from his throat. Before logical thought invaded the heavenly moment, his seed burst from him, pumping into his wife's willing body. Still, he continued to move inside her.

There was no going back now.

When he was done and spent, the realisation of what this meant forced him to roll onto his back and sigh.

Lord, never in his life had he felt so satisfied, so fulfilled. Such a level of peace banished his fears of fathering a child, of their future. Still, struggling to catch her breath, Priscilla lay at his side. Without thought, he placed a hand on her stomach. For some reason unbeknown, the image of her swollen with his child was not as terrifying as he imagined.

"Well, that was certainly worth the wait." Priscilla curled up against him, buried her face against his throat, draped her leg over his.

Matthew chuckled. Trust his wife to offer an honest appraisal. "While I have to agree, don't think we're to wait another week before trying it again. Give me ten minutes, and I'll be ready to continue."

"Ten minutes?" she purred. "Why so long?"

"Who would have thought an innocent would have the appetite of a seasoned seducer?"

She looked up at him. "It has nothing to do with the act and everything to do with being close to you." She came up to rest on her elbow, her other hand tracing a line over the hair on his chest. "I agreed to be honest with you—"

"Is this where you tell me I need to work on my technique?" Matthew snorted. "That you expected the moment to last a damn sight longer." As did he.

"No. It's where I tell you that I, too, am looking for the unique quality that speaks to my soul. And I think I've found it."

Intrigued as to what she found exceptional about his character, he probed further. "Is it loyalty? For I would never betray you, Priscilla."

"I know." The corners of her mouth curled up into a sweet smile. "It is many things, yet equally it is one perfect thing."

"Then it is trust and honesty, faith in general?"

"It is all of those and more." She pursed her lips, shrugged one shoulder and said, "It is love, Matthew. I have fallen in love with you."

He shouldn't have been shocked, but hearing the words aloud made them all the more real.

Panic flared.

He needed more time.

Showing not the slightest disappointment at his silent response, she placed a hand on his cheek. "Don't be afraid. It can't be helped. But it shouldn't change anything between us. I don't expect a declaration in return."

Still startled, it took a moment for him to speak. "Priscilla, I've spent a lifetime avoiding emotion." And for good reason. "I don't want to be the one to break your heart."

"You won't." Despite sounding confident, her hand slipped from his cheek. "Why would you when you've sworn to keep your promise? You'll always be loyal, honest and true. I ask no more of you than that."

A hundred questions flittered through his mind.

How was she able to give so freely? Why did she not feel the need to guard her delicate sensibilities? How was it she could love him when he'd given nothing in return?

One thing was certain. This lady deserved so much more than he could give.

Feeling a sudden desire to offer a small gesture in return, he said, "Come. I want to show you something." He climbed out of bed and dragged on his breeches, aware of her gaze scanning his naked body.

"Where are we going?"

"If I told you, then it wouldn't be a surprise."

She bit down on her bottom lip. "Will you come back here afterwards or are you to return to your own room?"

It took but a second to decide. "I think I might find something to entertain me in here."

"Then I am more than happy to oblige." She sat up but flopped back down. "Oh, I feel exhausted."

"And yet I did most of the work." The playful banter distracted his mind.

"Work? Was it such a chore?"

"You know damn well it wasn't." Being intimate with her

required little effort. "Now get dressed. It's cold in the attic, so you'll need a wrapper as well as your nightgown."

"The attic?" Curious, she sat up again and gave him her full attention. "Why do we need to go up there? Mrs Jacobs said there's nothing but old chests and broken furniture, that you keep the door locked."

"That's because I don't want anyone snooping around in there."

"If you're implying that I might—"

"I'm not talking about you. I don't want drunken lords rummaging through my belongings while trying to find a secluded place to do their business."

The thought of their house packed with a horde of brandy-swigging degenerates filled him with loathing. A few weeks ago he'd been happy to play host, had even boasted to Tristan of his ability to organise the best parties.

Now, it didn't matter how many times he bathed. Their dirt clung to his skin, seeped into his pores.

"Shall I bring a candle?" Priscilla's soft voice disturbed his reverie.

Matthew glanced up, noted she was already tying the belt on her wrapper and inwardly groaned for missing the pleasure of watching her dress.

"I'll carry the candle." The one in the lamp on the night stand nearest still had another hour or two before burning out. He took the lamp, opened the door and held out his hand to her. "It will be dark and dusty up there. We may even find a mouse or two."

They wouldn't find anything untoward. Mrs Jacobs inspected the room daily. But he liked the way Priscilla's small hand gripped his when nervous. Being master and protector gave him purpose. A job far more worthwhile than playing entertainer.

After entering his bedchamber to get the key, they worked their way up the stairs, mounting the narrow flight leading up to the fourth floor.

"Have you not thought to let the maids have their rooms up here?" she said. "It would be far warmer than the basement."

"When one hosts events for men with no morals, it is best that the servants remain together. Should there ever be a problem, a burly footman is never far away. Besides, where would I keep my work?"

"Your work?"

"My paintings." Matthew used the iron key to unlock the door at the top of the stairs. "It's dry up here, and the lack of light is an advantage." A studio would be preferable, somewhere to display his art. To exhibit at the Royal Academy would be better, but he was a practical man, not a dreamer.

"I didn't realise you kept your paintings in the attic." She entered the room, her narrow gaze flitting left and right in the darkness. "It's hard to see anything."

"Hold the lamp for a moment."

No sooner had she took the lamp than he ripped the sheets from the easels dotted about the room. Excitement, mixed with apprehension, made his heart beat faster.

Priscilla stepped closer and raised the lamp to study one landscape. Matthew watched her facial expressions intently. Surprise was the first emotion he noticed. The upward curl of her lips suggested she found the scene pleasant.

"I ... I don't know what to say." Hesitant fingers reached out stopping but an inch from the canvas. Wide eyes scanned the mountain range, the lake, the lush green trees in the foreground. "If heaven were on earth, it is how I imagine it would look. Is that a tower?" She pointed to the stone structure without doors or windows.

"It is," he said curtly for he had no desire to speak of the symbolic meaning behind his work. "Well?" His confidence faltered. Other than Priscilla, his work was the only thing he cared about. "Would you be happy to hang them on the wall in the drawing room?"

"Happy? I'd be ecstatic."

"Does that mean you approve?" If she thought he lacked skill, she would say so.

"Your talent leaves me speechless." She moved to the moonlit scene of a solitary man walking through a dark forest. "The figure looks so insignificant amidst the vast landscape, so alone, so sad." The sidelong glance she cast his way reflected the melancholic mood of his art. "Creative work often reflects a person's inner thoughts. Is that true in this case?"

A lump formed in Matthew's throat. "To an extent." The pictures were a gateway to his soul. He gestured to the lake painting. "Sometimes it is easy to lock oneself away in a tower and pretend that nothing beautiful exists beyond."

"Many people hide from their emotions. The darkness is their sanctuary." She nodded to the other canvas. "And what of the man in the forest?"

"Perhaps he is searching for a way out of the dark."

Now was not the time to discuss the past. To his mind, there was never a right time. Dragging the sheets off the floor, he draped them over the paintings, aware of her intense gaze boring into his back. But she said nothing.

When he'd finished the task, she came to stand at his side and placed a warm hand on his shoulder. "Do you paint anything other than landscapes?"

The question was a means to distract him; he knew that. Was she so attuned to his moods that she knew what he was thinking?

"I paint the things that rouse passion in my chest."

"Would you paint me?"

Sinful thoughts returned upon hearing the lascivious edge to her tone. "While you would be a subject I long to see staring back at me, any likeness of you would be for my own personal pleasure."

She sniggered. "You mean I would be stretched out naked on a bed of red silk, dangling a bunch of grapes over my mouth."

"Something like that." She knew him so well.

"Don't you need to get a picture in your mind's eye before you begin?"

From the way she touched her fingers to her collarbone, he could interpret her train of thought.

"A clear picture would be helpful. Perhaps you might spare some time to act as model and muse."

A soft hum left her lips. "I have time now." She reached for his hand and pulled him towards the door. "And I do so want to help you with your work."

CHAPTER 18

A rapturous melody filled the air. On the dance floor, joy graced the faces of the couples as they twirled about the candlelit ballroom. Gentlemen huddled in groups, partook in rowdy banter, cheered and raised their glasses in salute. Feminine giggles and shrieks indicated the amorous activities were well underway.

As always, the mood was one of fun and frivolity.

Matthew stood near the doors to the terrace, jaw clenched, and watched Lord Boden descend the steps into the crowded room. With a raised chin and disdainful pout, the man possessed Satan's arrogant air. Mr Parker-Brown scurried behind like an obedient disciple, inclining his head to those people Boden refused to acknowledge.

Since the fateful night at Lord Holbrook's card game, Mr Justin Travant was nowhere to be seen. Rumour was he'd taken a trip abroad. Either the man was overcome with remorse for his deceitful ways and sought to escape with his reputation intact, or Boden feared Travant's loose tongue and had forced him out of the country.

The rustling of silk behind him was accompanied by a soft

feminine sigh. Matthew swallowed a groan as he glanced over his shoulder.

"All alone and no one to play with?" Lucinda Pearce cast a sultry smile as she came to stand in front of him. One did not need to glance down to know that the bodice of her emerald-green gown barely covered her nipples.

"All alone and bored with your game." He hoped his blunt manner conveyed his indifference. But Lucinda was a woman used to cutting remarks, and so she moistened her lips as a sign she welcomed the challenge.

"Then perhaps it's time to change the rules. Perhaps you'll find I'm a partner willing to adapt." Miss Pearce breathed deeply and arched her back to better present her fleshy wares. "Or is your new toy still providing a modicum of entertainment?"

There was little point chastising her for her derogatory comment. She was immune to whip-like lashes of the tongue.

"New toys often become firm favourites, to where one couldn't bear to play with anything else. In that regard, they're irreplaceable, utterly unique, loved beyond measure."

Had he said *loved*? He'd meant to say *cherished*.

Lucinda's confident gaze faltered, but she quickly recovered. "There's no need to pretend. I hear the croak in your voice when you speak of love. A man with your voracious appetite couldn't possibly settle with one woman."

A few weeks ago he might have agreed. But things were different now. Priscilla had penetrated his protective shield. If he closed his eyes and slowed his breathing, he could feel her essence burning bright inside. It never left him.

"You assume I still hunger for meaningless conquests." Lord, how had he found pleasure in such vacuous pursuits? "Perhaps I have found something more substantial to sate my craving. Perhaps such depth of fulfilment means I shall never feel famished again."

Lucinda snorted. "I don't believe a word of it." The tip of her tongue traced the seam of her lips, and she placed her palm flat on his chest. "Why trot on a pony when you can gallop bareback on a stallion? We all know you like to ride hard."

Matthew stepped back. "If you knew me at all, you would not have used that analogy. I hate horses and only use them when the need arises. And so I shall turn your question on its head. Why would a man want to ride a filthy, sweaty beast when he can ride in a clean, exquisitely made carriage?"

Miss Pearce found the decency to gasp.

"Now," Matthew continued, "I don't know about you, but I'm tired of trading quips and avoiding direct answers. So, let me give it to you plainly. I am not interested in a liaison. The only woman I will ever bed is my wife."

"You can't be serious. What, you'd not even be open to oral favours?"

Damn. Did the woman not understand the word *no*!

"Despite the reckless antics of many reprobates, I've yet to revoke a guest's membership. Yours could well be the first. Find another gentleman to please. Your efforts are wasted on me. Are we clear?"

Lucinda sucked in her cheeks. "Crystal."

Despite her nod of agreement, there was a look of determination about her countenance that suggested otherwise. Indeed, her exaggerated pout was that of a woman who always got her own way.

Equally intent on ruining his evening, Lord Boden sidled up beside them. "Ah, Chandler. I hate to spoil your little *tête-à-tête*, but I was wondering where I might find your wife." A sly smirk was followed by a flash of disdain as he glanced briefly at Miss Pearce. "I can see you're occupied, and as we have an hour until the card game begins, I thought Mrs Chandler might like to dance."

Like a flame to a barn full of straw, anger sparked to life in Matthew's chest. "My wife dances with no one but me." He didn't care if the whole world thought him controlling and possessive.

Boden sneered. "Thankfully, the lady appears to have a mind of her own. When she discovers you cavorting with one of your guests, perhaps she might seek a distraction. As a man who appreciates the finer things in life, I would happily oblige."

A growl rumbled in the back of Matthew's throat. One more word from the smug bastard and fists would be flying. "Lay a finger on my wife, and I'll call you out. If I were you, I'd have a care. I'm at my most nimble at dawn."

"I can vouch for that," Miss Pearce added.

"You might have a different view once I've taken your wager and left you penniless." Boden tugged at his fancy cuffs and brushed a hand through his mop of dark hair. "And when I call in your vowels, what will you do then? Desperate men often have no choice but to sell the things most precious to them."

What the blazes was Boden suggesting? "You mean there is something I possess that you wish to buy?"

"Precisely. Of course we could forgo the card game, and I could return your vowel as payment. That way we both benefit. And it will give you an opportunity to spend time with your friend Miss Pearce."

Lucinda inclined her head. "How generous of you to think of me, my lord," she said, though her tone held a hint of contempt.

Bile bubbled in Matthew's gut. Surely Boden was not speaking of Priscilla. "I have no inclination to spend time with Miss Pearce, but I'll hear your offer all the same."

Boden gave a dandified wave. "Running an establishment like this, no doubt you're party to many business transactions. As a member, I would pay an extortionate sum to spend one night with your wife."

Darkness descended.

Faster than a man could blink, Matthew grabbed the snooty lord by his cravat and yanked it hard. "You arrogant bastard. I'll see you in hell if you so much as look at my wife in the wrong way."

Arms flailing, Boden coughed and spluttered, his eyes bulging from shock rather than lack of air. With claw-like fingers, he tried to release Matthew's grip but to no avail.

With the strength of ten men, Matthew was determined to hold on. "Know that I do not take kindly to threats."

"Let him go," Lucinda whispered, pulling at his hand, too. "People are staring."

"Do you think I give a damn what these people think?"

A lady cleared her throat. "This is not the time or place to air one's grievances." The calm, familiar voice caught Matthew's attention. Priscilla stepped into the fold and placed a comforting hand on his forearm. "Release Lord Boden before he chokes to death."

Matthew ground his teeth and stared down his nose at Boden. "Disrespect my wife again, and I'll kill you."

Judging by the collective gasp, it seemed he'd made his point.

With a disdainful snort, Matthew released Boden's silk cravat and brushed his hands to convey his contempt. Still, his fists throbbed with the need to punch his aquiline nose until flat.

"Assumptions were made based on the nature of our business. I'm certain Lord Boden did not mean to offend," Priscilla said. "If he did, that would make him extremely foolish, and he does not strike me as a man who wants people to think him a fool."

Boden sucked in a breath, straightened his attire and after a few groans and grumbles resumed a dignified air. "Forgive me." He turned to Priscilla and bowed gracefully although his greedy gaze devoured her. "I meant no disrespect. On the contrary, I am a man who admires perfection in all things. Any insult was aimed at your husband, and him alone."

As the anger clouding Matthew's vision slowly dissipated, he turned to Priscilla. Dressed in a sapphire-blue gown with an entic-ingly low-cut bodice, she looked magnificent. His eyes weren't the only ones drawn to the jewelled brooch nestled between the curve of her breasts.

"I'm afraid your compliment is unfounded, my lord," Priscilla replied, and Boden was forced to look at her face. "You see, like my husband, I am far from perfect. Indeed, I fear we share the same unpredictability when threatened. I am just as likely to display unladylike bouts of violence and anger at the mere thought of another woman laying a hand on him." Priscilla's coy gaze swept over Lucinda. "Ah, Miss Pearce, good evening. I would apologise for my husband's aggressive display, but I assume you're accustomed to ungentlemanly behaviour."

Lucinda smiled weakly. "And why would you assume that?"

With an indolent wave, Priscilla gestured to the crowd. "One does not attend parties such as these when possessed with delicate sensibilities."

"Is that why you're rarely in attendance?" Lucinda lifted her chin. "Do our amorous activities offend you?"

Sickened by the depths of their depravity and ashamed of his association, Matthew contemplated throwing everyone out.

"No, your activities do not offend me," Priscilla replied. "But while passion is a thing to be celebrated, I prefer to honour my vows and focus my energy on one person as opposed to many." She placed her hand in the crook of Matthew's arm. "Now, if you will excuse us. I find I'm in need of air."

Priscilla drew him out onto the terrace. Due to the early hour, the garden was deserted. The ladies were busy playing coquette, the gentlemen acting the lothario although there was nothing deceptive about their goals to seduce.

Matthew sucked in a breath. The sky was clear, and the cool breeze calmed his heated blood. For a moment they stared out over the manicured lawn, each silent and lost in their own thoughts.

Guilt, like a twisted vine, crawled through his body, creeping, crushing, until he could no longer contain the emotion.

Matthew turned to face Priscilla but struggled to look into her eyes. "How can you have any respect for me when I bring these people into our home? Why do you not judge me, condemn my actions, curse me to the Devil?"

She gave a weak smile and put her hand on his cheek. "Because I promised to obey you. I promised to stand by your side through life's trials and tribulations, to trust you. Because you never gave me a choice."

The last comment hit him hard. The truth was as painful as a knife to the heart.

"I've made a mess of things." There was a part of him that did not want to acknowledge his failures. Ignorance was often bliss. "I've undermined the foundation of our relationship, demanding honesty but only when it serves my purpose."

Her hand slipped from his cheek. "The questions you asked were the ones you thought important."

That was the point. At no time had he considered her feelings.

"Then I'm asking you to be honest with me now. Truly honest." Other people's opinions didn't matter, yet he knew her criticism would cut deep. "Do not spare me. Do not fear reprisal."

"Very well." She swallowed, inhaled and exhaled slowly. "I hate having these people here. A lady should feel safe at home, not worry about a randy lord finding his way into her bedchamber. Just hearing their lustful cries, watching them defile our ... well." A long, drawn-out sigh left her lips. "You're worth so much more than this. Some things are more important than money."

For the first time in his life, he had to agree.

"Money was not the only motivation." He'd hoped people would come to depend on him, to need what he could provide. "Though loath to admit it, these people were like my family."

"I'm sure you don't need me to point out the obvious flaws in your logic."

"No. In truth, you are the only person I can depend upon." Melancholy infused his tone, and he mentally shook himself. "I should have knocked Boden's teeth down his throat for what he said."

"And what good would that do? We need to handle Lord Boden with care until we've won back your vowel."

"There's a chance we might lose. I'll not ask my brother for money, and so it would mean raising a loan against this house."

She shrugged. "If that is what Fate has in store, who are we to argue?"

Priscilla had a way of infusing an element of calm into any situation. When it came to the card game, there was another option though his pride refused to accept it was a possibility.

"We could choose not to play and simply repay the ten thousand I owe." God, he'd spent weeks dreaming about wiping the smug grin off Boden's face.

A grim look settled around her mouth. "In all honesty, I'm not certain my uncle has the funds to pay my dowry. No legal documents were ever drawn up. Now I fear his word is not his bond, and you have married me under false pretences."

Would her uncle be dishonourable enough to renege?

The thought had crossed Matthew's mind. From what he'd discovered of the lord's recent antics, Callan was struggling to keep his creditors at bay. The fact Callan owed Boden such a large sum also proved worrying. Perhaps Boden would use the debt to bribe Priscilla.

Matthew shook the thought from his head. It was better to focus on one problem at a time than invent scenarios that had not yet happened.

"My reasons for marrying you no longer matter." Whether he received her dowry or not, one thing was clear. "I don't care about the money. In time you might not agree, but our foolish, rather rash decision to wed has brought far greater rewards."

She placed her hand on his chest. "Are you saying you're happy you have a wife?"

"I'm saying I'm happy I have you in my life." The sudden

urge to show his appreciation took hold, and he brushed her lips in a tender kiss far removed from the lust-fuelled ones they'd shared of late. "I'll do whatever you suggest. We can play, or we can walk away. I can continue to host these lewd parties, or I can tell them all to go to the devil. As my wife, I'm giving you the choice."

Without a word, she touched her lips to his and kissed him with the fiery passion he knew burned bold and bright inside. Desire sparked instantly though for them it always simmered below the surface when in each other's company.

"There is only one way to proceed if we are ever to be truly happy," she said, breaking contact. "We will play the card game. Neither of us will rest until we stop Lord Boden's fraudulent activities. My conscience requires that I do something."

"And if we lose, what then?"

"Then you will take a loan. Together, we will continue to host these parties until it is repaid. Sell your paintings and seek commission to paint more."

"Sell my paintings?" The thought caused a sharp pang in his chest.

"You cannot hide them in the dark forever."

"Who on earth would want to buy them?"

She tutted. "Many people. Really, for a man who oozes confidence, I'm surprised at your lack of faith. From what I saw, your work is remarkable."

The compliment nurtured self-belief and banished all doubts, albeit temporarily.

"And what are we to do if we win?"

"Sell your paintings and seek commission to paint more," she repeated as though the answer was obvious. "Only when you answer the call of your heart, will you feel fulfilled."

Hearing her wise words caused a warm glow in his chest. A tingling sensation followed, trickled through every part of his body. While he was always ready to bed her, this felt different.

Dare he say it, he needed her. How the hell had he survived on his own?

Was it love? He had no notion.

Everything reminded him of her. The sound of trickling water when he washed always brought to mind her terrified face as she hid in the shadows by Holbrook's fountain. He'd never be able to ride in a carriage again without recalling the pleasure she'd given him. Oysters roused an image of her full lips. The rain. Dancing. Anything red.

It all came back to her.

"As always I cannot argue with your logic." Lacking the courage to put his feelings into words, he held his hand out to her. "Shall we give the gossips something juicy to savour? Shall we take our place at the card table?"

"I have a few ideas on that score if you're happy to trust my judgement."

"Of course." He inclined his head. "Together we make a formidable opponent. Let us teach Boden a lesson he'll never forget."

CHAPTER 19

The parlour was set aside for those men who liked to gamble with money as opposed to a woman's affections. Rumours of the wager between Matthew and Lord Boden had spread through the throng. Indeed, the guests piled into the dimly lit room, squashed and squeezed into every available space in the hope of witnessing the event. Consequently, the room was hot. The pungent odour of stale tobacco and cheap perfume tainted the air. The sickly sweet smell of liquor made Priscilla want to retch.

"Heaven help us if there's a fire," Priscilla said, moving around the table to take the seat opposite Matthew. Lord Boden held out her chair despite Matthew's mutterings of disapproval. "Thank you, my lord. I hope you will be as generous when we beat you at whist."

Boden chuckled though a smile barely formed on his lips. "While I am more than confident in my ability to succeed, your optimism is refreshing. Indeed, there are not many ladies who—"

"Stop harassing my wife with your sentimental nonsense." Matthew removed his coat and draped it over the back of the chair. "She can see through your amiable facade."

"What you deem a facade is simply good manners," Boden countered though there was a hint of amusement in his tone, a reluctance to offend.

"You must excuse my husband," Priscilla said, trying not to show she found the lord abhorrent. "His mood will be much improved once he wins back his vowel."

"When I win, I shall be ecstatic," Matthew snapped.

"Determination is an admirable quality," Boden replied. "But you cannot hope to win. I excel at the game. There is no finer player in all of London. Ask around."

Good. She'd cast a line to lure this big fish. Now Boden had taken a nibble it wouldn't be too difficult to reel him in.

"Perhaps you exaggerate your skill, my lord. Perhaps your confidence is merely a mask to rouse fear in our hearts. After all, did you not lose at The Diamond Club last night?"

Excited murmurs drifted through the crowd.

"We lost, but the mistake was mine," Mr Parker-Brown interjected as he took the final seat. "I can assure you, madam, it won't happen again."

"A mistake?" The faint look of suspicion passed over Matthew's face. It would not do to alert Boden that they suspected foul play. Besides, Priscilla wanted to use this opportunity to gain a pledge from the pompous lord and his partner.

Casting Matthew an inconspicuous look to be cautious, Priscilla said, "Precisely my point. Mistakes happen, my lord. While I admire your confidence, you cannot be assured of success tonight."

As expected, Boden rose to the challenge. "Madam, I can assure you, *losing* is not a word I'm familiar with." His gaze dropped to the brooch sewn onto her gown, scanned her exposed flesh. "I always get what I want."

Arrogance was to be Lord Boden's downfall.

"Then you should have no objection showing your benevolence. A gesture of goodwill will convince me of your generous nature and reinforce your assertion that you possess great expertise."

"A gesture of goodwill?" Boden repeated, the slight tremor in his voice was accompanied by a deep line between his brows. "What are you suggesting?"

Priscilla steeled herself. "Have faith in your conviction. Make my uncle's vowel part of the wager."

Matthew cleared his throat. "I cannot cover your uncle's vowel if we lose."

Priscilla smiled. "Lord Boden need ask for nothing in return. If we lose, we shall simply pay the agreed amount. If we win, he will return both vowels. Being so highly skilled it will not be a great risk." She looked up at the gaping crowd. "And does that not make for a worthier wager?"

Mumbled words of approval rumbled through the parlour.

Lord Boden scanned the horde of excited faces. To reject the idea would make him appear weak, a man who boasts but lacks substance. And that simply wouldn't do.

"Very well." The nerve in Lord Boden's cheek twitched. "Should we lose, both vowels shall be returned though I can assure you that will not be the case."

Mr Parker-Brown made an odd puffing noise. "Shouldn't you consult me before—"

"The decision is made," Boden snapped. "Mrs Chandler may trust that I will honour our bargain. That she alone has the ability to elicit my compassion for her uncle's plight."

Matthew grabbed the pack of cards from the centre of the card table and began shuffling them as though they had slighted him in some way.

"The excitement gleaned from taking a risk is sometimes its own reward, my lord. But I thank you for your kindness and pray you accept defeat with equal grace." She waved her hand over the green cloth surface, hoping the tremble in her fingers wasn't evident. "Shall we proceed with the game?"

"Do you wish to appoint a dealer, Lord Boden?" Matthew placed the cards on the table. "One of the gentlemen in the crowd, perhaps?"

"We know each other well enough to trust that one of us may deal."

"Then I would prefer you accept the task." Matthew pushed the deck towards him. "I'd hate for you to lose and then accuse me of cheating."

"There are enough witnesses here to attest to honest play."

Heavens, the gentleman's hypocrisy knew no bounds.

Boden shuffled the cards without argument and presented the pack to Priscilla. "The lady may cut the deck to choose the trump card."

"How kind of you, my lord." Cutting the cards roughly half-way, she revealed the five of hearts to the gentlemen at the table, and the spectators gathered around. "The suit of one in search of perfect love. The ruler of home and family."

Matthew smiled. "Then it was an apt choice."

"Let's hope Fate bestows a bounty of luck upon me."

Boden gave an irritated sigh as he reshuffled and dealt the cards. "Before we begin, we should clarify the rules of play. Thirteen tricks to a hand. One point for every trick earned over six. The first team to reach five points win a game. The best of three games win the match. Agreed?"

"Agreed" came their collective response.

"I recall seeing a decanter of port when I wandered in here earlier." Lord Boden craned his neck though it was impossible to see anything beyond the wall of people. "As host shouldn't you offer us all a drink, Chandler?"

"You may partake in a tipple, though I must decline."

"Nonsense. In testament to the friendly spirit of the game, we must all drink together." Boden glanced at Priscilla. "Surely, you will take a nip of port with me, something to quell the nerves."

"After your generous offer to return my uncle's vowel should we win, it would be rude to refuse."

"My wife has no need to satisfy your whims." Matthew's defiant green eyes flashed with hatred.

"There is no need for concern." She remained resolute. "You may trust my judgement. A small drop of port will do no harm."

Gesturing to the waiting footman, Priscilla instructed him to bring the decanter and glasses. The servant placed the crystal vessel on the small trestle table at their side and began pouring. Matthew's curious gaze scanned the unfamiliar decanter.

What, did he really think she'd be foolish enough to fall prey to Boden's scheming? A few drops of laudanum would cloud her judgement enough to make mistakes in the game. A few drops would diminish her ability to stop the lecherous lord from making an amorous advance should the need take him.

"Instead of port, I wonder if I may have brandy." Boden's desire to drink something other than the drink he'd tampered with was not surprising. "You'd prefer brandy wouldn't you Parker?"

The red-haired gentleman nodded. "Too much port gives me gout."

"Well my husband shall join me in a glass, and you gentlemen shall enjoy a brandy."

They all accepted their respective glasses. Matthew stared at her as he brought it to his lips.

"Trust me," she reiterated. It was a lot to ask from a man who trusted no one. "The liquor will have no effect on your ability to play." She turned to Boden. "Many a drunk has played carelessly at the tables."

Boden snorted. "Indeed, hence it's only right we all take a drink."

The sneaky scoundrel.

It took a tremendous effort not to jump up and punch him on the nose.

Little did he know that she'd watched him enter the room

when he thought no one was looking. Having learnt that he'd drugged the port at Holbrook's card game, and that he'd presume port would be her choice over brandy, she'd arranged for both decanters to be changed. On Anne's advice, the small amount of laudanum she'd added to the brandy would be enough to muddle the arrogant lord's mind.

After raising their glasses in a salute to Fate, the game began.

Boden's tactic in all previous games was to let his opponents win the first few tricks. As per their earlier conversation, Priscilla was to play low, particularly if playing her strongest suit, while Matthew would divert suspicion and mix up the play.

Priscilla and Matthew won the first four tricks—Boden and Parker-Brown the next four. The slight movements of hand and face were harder to detect when seated around the table. To stare at the men during play would seem odd. With so much at stake, the pressure to focus took tremendous effort. Indeed, the tension in the air was like a heavy weight pressing down on her shoulders.

When they lost the next hand, Priscilla sensed her husband's frustration and knew that they had no choice but to concentrate on their own game.

But how was she to communicate her intentions?

Matthew's growl of disapproval when they lost the next hand gave her the opportunity she needed.

"Your mind is too distracted," she said. "It is easy to analyse the game when watching from the crowd. To be in the midst makes it harder to anticipate how one's opponents might play."

"Perhaps it's the port." Matthew nodded to the footman who removed his glass.

Boden chuckled and swallowed a mouthful of his brandy. "Can't take your liquor? Perhaps it's time to accept you have no skill at cards."

"Ignore Lord Boden," Priscilla interjected before her husband leapt across the table and throttled the man. "He is simply trying to put you off your game. There is no need to look at anyone else here but me." Their eyes locked. She arched a brow, exaggerated the movement in the hope he would read her silent communication. "Like the queen of hearts, I hope to have a favourable influence."

One corner of Matthew's mouth twitched. He rubbed his cheek, pressed his fingers together in the sign used by Boden and his ilk. "Then as your king, I welcome your assistance."

Excellent.

He understood her meaning perfectly.

They continued playing, Priscilla using the breathing technique to convey the numbered cards, the slight movements to indicate the face cards. Boden and Mr Parker-Brown were too concerned with watching each other to notice anything untoward.

Counting the cards took concentration. But being the first to reach five points, they won the first game.

"It seems your luck is improving, Chandler." Mr Mullworth tapped Matthew on the shoulder. The portly gentleman raised his chin to acknowledge Mr Parker-Brown. "You know what they say. Trouble comes in threes. There's every chance you could lose again this evening."

Members of the crowd jeered.

"Enough with your blabbering," Lord Boden chided. The whites of his eyes carried a hint of pink. The pupils contracted to tiny black dots. The rigid line of his jaw had softened. "Only when you find the courage to play are you worthy of passing comment." Snatching the brandy glass off the table, he downed the contents in such a way as to show his disdain. "Now let's get on with the blasted game."

Mullworth hung his head and shrank back into the crowd.

"Are you well?" Mr Parker-Brown shuffled uncomfortably in his seat. The man had taken but three sips of his drink and looked at his partner with an air of bewilderment. "Why don't we stretch our legs before we reconvene?"

"You speak as though I'm infirm. Now be quiet and let me deal the bloody cards."

Boden practically threw the cards at them and was forced to reshuffle and start again when a few flipped face up. This time he didn't bother to ask Priscilla to pick the trump card but followed the rule that last one dealt denoted the key suit.

Priscilla examined her hand and glanced up at Matthew. "Are you ready to win another game?"

A mischievous grin formed on his lips. "You know me. I'm always ready."

The first few tricks were always the hardest to win. The more cards played, the easier it was to work out what was left. Matthew and Priscilla won the first hand, Boden the second and third. Come the fourth hand, the lord's movements were slower. Judging by Parker-Brown's mumbled moans, they were struggling with the language of silent communication.

And so it went on, trick after trick.

"Winning this trick gives us five points and means we've won the game." Matthew's voice whilst conveying a hint of loathing, smouldered with satisfaction.

"I can damn well count," Boden snapped. "You sound like a bloody governess determined to make a point."

Parker-Brown's bottom lip wobbled. "I trust you were not relying on Mr Chandler's promissory note to pay creditors."

"Of course not." Lord Boden's cheeks puffed and glowed red. "Do you take me for one of these debauched fools?"

Members of the crowd gasped at the lord's audacity. Muttered curses breezed through the room. The air was heavy with disdain though no one openly challenged his comment.

Matthew leant over the table towards Lord Boden. "It's your turn to play."

The card quivered in Boden's fingers. Still, his cruel mouth formed an arrogant curl. "Let's see if you can beat the knave of hearts." He threw the card onto the table, sat back and folded his arms across his chest.

From what Priscilla had counted, and from reading the signs, Matthew had the nine of hearts. When he threw it down, Boden gave a mocking snort. The spectators in the front row sighed with disappointment.

"It seems your confidence is misplaced," Lord Boden derided.

"Thankfully, a trick requires four cards, not two," Matthew countered.

"Mr Parker-Brown," Priscilla prompted. "It is your turn to play."

The man's nervous gaze flicked about the room. The three of clubs fell from his grasp and landed on the table.

"Bloody idiot." Boden was far from pleased.

Priscilla fought hard to hide any sign of emotion. She stared at the card in her hand, her vision growing hazy, her mind playing its own tricks.

A tense silence filled the room. Fifty pairs of eyes watched and waited.

"As the lady of the house, it seems fitting that this should be the last card of play." Allowing a wide grin to form, she placed the queen of hearts on top of the pile. "It seems that a woman's love is the key to success."

Matthew's green eyes shone brightly. "I trust you are right."

Mr Parker-Brown bowed his head.

Boden snatched the queen off the table, flipped it over in his fingers and then held it up to examine it further. "You can't have won." The Devil's own fury filled Boden's eyes. He waved at the footman. "Pour me a large brandy while I examine the cards."

Many men booed and jeered.

"They've won, Boden. They've beat you."

"Accept your fate with good grace," another shouted.

Matthew pushed out of the chair. Wearing a smug grin, he said, "I shall expect both my and Lord Callan's vowels returned as a matter of urgency. There can be no doubt as to the winners of this game."

A rapturous applause rang out. One gentleman after another approached the table to offer their congratulations.

"Damn good game, Chandler."

"We knew you had him after the first few hands."

Matthew placed his hand on his chest. "I cannot take all the credit."

"Like all the best fillies, your wife pipped him to the post," Lord Parson said.

"Indeed." Matthew glanced at her. The look of admiration in his eyes stole her breath. "In this house, it is the queen who reigns supreme."

CHAPTER 20

The overwhelming sense of satisfaction flowing through Matthew's veins had sated his hunger for revenge. Boden would do one of two things. Had he any sense, he would shrink back into the shadows, go about his business never to darken Matthew's door again. Equally, he could rant and rave about the unfairness of it all, swear they'd cheated and a host of other annoying things just to cause trouble.

Perhaps he should have thrown Boden and Parker-Brown out onto the street. Then again, looking at the lord's solemn face for the rest of the evening would bring immense pleasure. Plenty of other gentlemen would find amusement in the sombre sight, too.

One thing was certain. Swigging the last of the brandy had dulled the lord's aggressive nature. Abandoned by Parker-Brown, Boden still sat at the card table, drowning his sorrows.

Upon entering the ballroom with Priscilla on his arm, Matthew noted the opening strains of a waltz. "Shall we dance, Priscilla? Shall we show these people how perfect we are together?"

She glanced at him, a smile illuminating her whole face. "Dancing with you would be a fitting end to a wonderful night."

They found a space on the floor, and he pulled her into an embrace. "I can promise you one thing. This dance will not signify the end of the evening. Hours of pleasure still await us."

A faint blush touched her cheeks. Despite sharing many passionate exchanges, there was still an element of innocence about her countenance he found endearing.

"We have much to celebrate," she said as they locked fingers. "I'll never forget the look on your face when I played the queen."

The mere mention of it caused another rush of excitement, a feeling intensified by the feel of his wife's body as he twirled her around the room. "Did you see Boden's face? The man came here intending to bleed me dry. What I want to know is what happened to the decanter of port?"

"Well," she began with a coy grin, "I noticed him enter the parlour. Just from his shifty manner, I knew he was up to mischief. And after what you said about him drugging the port at Lord Holbrook's soiree, I suspected he'd planned a similar trick."

"And so what did you do?"

"I told John to throw the port away, to replace the decanter with the one from the drawing room."

"For a man adept at observing signals, I'm surprised Boden didn't notice the difference between a square and a tulip decanter."

"He was in and out of the parlour so quickly I doubt he gave the shape of the vessel much thought. Besides, he was more interested in the brandy."

Matthew chuckled. While Boden had mocked him for his inability to hold liquor, the pompous oaf had downed three quarters of the decanter. "Brandy proved to be his downfall. After the second glass, he was struggling to focus. And he had the temerity to taunt me."

A sly smile formed on her lips. "Well, it might not have been the brandy that clouded his thoughts."

With his curiosity piqued, he pulled her closer and lowered his head so his mouth was but an inch from her ear. "Have you been naughty, Priscilla?"

"A little, though it was Anne who supplied the laudanum."

"You drugged him?"

"I knew he wouldn't drink the port."

Matthew threw his head back and laughed. "Heavens, where would I be without you?"

She raised her chin. "You'd be twenty thousand pounds in debt, miserable, bored with playing host to a bunch of degenerates. You would only have one friend instead of two."

"Is that what we are? Friends as well as lovers?"

"We are all things to each other—confidante, companion, partner in crime."

"Now we've mastered the language of the card sharps, you realise we could earn quite a substantial sum of money if we toured the gaming hells."

"You won't have time for cards."

"Why? Have you thought of a better way for me to spend my time?"

She moistened her lips. "The activity I had in mind will keep you busy for hours. The pleasure gleaned will be so intense it will soothe your soul."

While his body responded instantly to the seductive lilt in her voice, he suspected she spoke of something other than passionate encounters in the bedchamber.

"As a man with a wicked mind, there is only one activity I can think of, yet I suspect you mean something else entirely."

"Oh, I intend to find new ways to pleasure your body, but I was speaking about painting. If you're to have a gallery, you will need more than three pieces of work."

The fear of failure was often stifling. With his work kept hidden in the attic, no one could judge or offer the scathing criticism that would make him refuse to pick a brush up again.

"How is it you make an unsurmountable task appear easily achievable?" he said.

"Because I've seen your work, and I believe in you."

His heart skipped a beat. Time stopped for a moment. No one had ever said those words to him. When he shook himself back to the present, a well of emotion rose from his chest to block his throat.

"Priscilla ... I ..."

The music stopped. Damn. Other couples left the floor, but he stood and stared into her blue eyes. A multitude of words raced through his mind but expressing emotion never came easy.

She must have sensed his torment. With no regard for the other people in the room, she raised her lips to his. The kiss was slow, sweet, satisfied him in a way he'd not thought possible whilst still fully clothed.

"We can talk about the future once Boden's returned your vowel," she said, pulling away. "Now I shall leave you to work. No doubt your guests want to congratulate you on the outcome of the game."

"Stay." That one word told a story. It was a tale of a man who trusted no one, who gave nothing, a man redeemed by the love of a perfect woman.

"If I thought I might have you all to myself, then I would." She placed her palm on his chest. "Can you not request they leave early?"

"I'd have a better chance of finding a one-ended stick."

She chuckled. "Then I shall unlock the connecting door and wait patiently."

He pulled his watch from his waistcoat pocket and checked the time. "Give me an hour, two at most."

"Take as long as you need. I'm not going anywhere."

Part of him wanted to keep her at his side, to talk, to dance. Part of him wanted her far away from those libertines skilled enough to lure her into a dark corner or empty room.

"Then let me escort you to the stairs."

Cutting through the crowd, they made their way into the hall.

Matthew turned to John who was standing as straight as a pencil by the newel post. "Mrs Chandler is going to bed." And he wished he was going with her. "You're to remain here until all the guests have left. No one is allowed upstairs. Is that clear?"

Boden was too inebriated to be any trouble tonight, but still, a strange sense of foreboding gripped him. Would the lord seek a liaison with Priscilla purely as a means of revenge?

"Regardless of the circumstances, you're not to leave your post," Matthew reiterated.

John bowed. "I understand, sir."

"I'll be perfectly fine." Priscilla touched his arm. "Now hurry. You have two hours to get rid of this rabble."

Matthew took her hand, brought it to his lips and pressed a kiss on her knuckles. "You were amazing tonight."

Witnessing her radiant smile was the most satisfying part of the whole evening.

"We were amazing," she said. Brushing one final kiss across his lips, she climbed the stairs to her bedchamber.

God, he was a jumbled bag of emotions. His heart hammered against his ribs. Did it stem from his eagerness to join her or the sudden fear of losing the only damn thing that mattered? The fluttering in his stomach was an entirely new sensation.

If John thought it odd that Matthew was still gaping at the stairs long after he'd heard Priscilla close her door, he gave no indication.

"I'll not move until the last guest has left, sir," John said. There was a brief pause. "Is everything all right, sir?"

"Yes, John. Everything is fine." Matthew sighed and dragged his hand down his face. "Life can be surprising. It can take but one event to send you spiralling on a different course."

A deep frown lined John's brow.

"It's like getting on the wrong mail coach at an inn," Matthew continued, trying to help the footman understand. "Your first instinct is to panic. You feel lost, helpless. But then at some point on the journey, you realise it was the right one all along."

"Yes, sir," John said, but probably hadn't got the first clue what Matthew was rambling on about.

Leaving John to concentrate on his duties, Matthew returned to the ballroom. He would begin his mission to empty the house by dropping a few discreet hints in Lord Parson's ear. But the blasted man had disappeared.

Chigwell, Mullworth and Mrs Wilson were conversing near the terrace, and so he thought to try there.

"Lord, watching you wipe the grin off Boden's face was the highlight of the evening." Chigwell slapped Matthew on the back. "Parker-Brown scurried off into the night, his chin dragging the floor."

"I imagine he has rushed home to assess his accounts," Mrs Wilson remarked with a cackle.

"You must be in the mood for celebrating," Chigwell said. "Let's play a drinking game."

Bloody hell. If they consumed any more brandy, they were liable to make a mess of the floor. "With a little over an hour left until I must bid you all good night, I think your time would be better served mingling."

That was a polite way of saying "find someone to fuck and then begone". As the vulgar remark formed in his mind, a wave of disgust swept over him. He was tired of playing parent to the weak and perverted.

"An hour?" Mullworth moaned. "That doesn't give a man much time." With an open mouth, he scoured the crowd. "Damn. There's no one here who takes my fancy."

Mrs Wilson nudged the slack-jawed devil. "Oh, there must be someone you've had your eye on. Someone who gets the old blood boiling. And don't look at me. I choose my men as I do my meat."

Chigwell chuckled. "What, you mean thick with a juicy covering of fat?"

"No, you fool." Mrs Wilson hit Chigwell's forearm with her folded fan. "I mean young, lean and tender."

Matthew feigned amusement. "As the average age of the gentlemen in here must be forty, I'd say you're out of luck."

"I'd say we are all out of luck." Mullworth's eyes widened as he spotted someone amongst the sea of heads. "Then again, it seems Chandler here might be the only one guaranteed a jolly time this evening."

Matthew followed Mullworth's gaze to the woman approaching. Like a snake slithering through the grass, Lucinda Pearce weaved through the crowd. She joined them, her forked tongue flicking over her lips as she scanned Matthew from head to toe.

"You know Chandler is closing the doors early tonight," Mullworth grumbled for the umpteenth time.

"Early? But he can't." Lucinda trailed her fingers over the neckline of her bodice. "The night has barely begun. Is a win at the tables not cause for celebration?"

It was. But he intended to commemorate the moment in private.

Mullworth sighed. "I don't suppose you'd forgo a dalliance with Chandler and bring a desperate man some comfort?"

"Of course not." Lucinda's sharp tone quickly mellowed. "But it wouldn't hurt to hear your proposition. At the very least, I might find someone else who interests you." Lucinda turned to Matthew. She wore the same sultry grin he'd seen a hundred times before. "Don't go anywhere, Chandler. I shall be right back."

Lucinda sauntered off with Mullworth. With any luck, she'd find someone else to stalk, someone else to stare at with her beady eyes. Indeed, his patience for her games had reached an end.

Mullworth's comment irritated him, too. It didn't matter how affectionate he was with his wife. People still assumed he would frolic with the likes of Miss Pearce. Tales and gossip had no effect on him, but the last thing he wanted was to hurt Priscilla.

Perhaps the time had come to focus on more worthy pursuits. To progress one had to reassess one's priorities. Painting was his love. So why the hell was he wasting time entertaining degenerates? People who vilified his home and abused his character.

"Chandler. Are you so drunk you've lost the use of your faculties?" Chigwell's amused voice disturbed his reverie. "Did you not hear what I said?"

"Forgive me. No." Matthew looked up and noted Chigwell was alone.

"We're leaving." He slapped Matthew on the back. "I'm to give Mrs Wilson a ride home whereupon she is to make a thorough assessment of my person and decide if mature beef is just as tasty as veal."

"Then for your sake, I hope you come up to scratch."

Chigwell patted him on the back. "I intend to suck in my stomach and give it my best effort."

In his eagerness to reach Mrs Wilson, who was waiting on the stairs, Chigwell rushed off. But Matthew was not left alone for long.

"And so you find yourself without friends again, Matthew," Lucinda mocked. "Perhaps you should make more effort to nurture relationships."

"What's wrong, Lucinda? Are you tired of Mullworth already?"

"Mullworth is hardly what one would call a virile specimen of a man, whereas you radiate strength and a powerful, masculine energy. Indeed, it is the reason I have decided to give you one more chance. There is a comfortable sofa in the parlour, I recall. And you would be surprised what we could achieve in an hour."

For the love of God, the snake had shed her skin and had no recollection of their earlier conversation.

"How many times must I tell you? I love my wife." The truth hit him so hard he jerked his head. Bloody hell. "I love my wife," he repeated with a slight hint of surprise as his mouth curled up into a smile. "There is not a woman on earth who could tempt me to be unfaithful."

Lucinda drew back ready to spit venom. "Then you're a fool, a damn cuckold. I've seen the way she dances with men."

"No, you've seen the way she dances with her husband."

"I've seen the way she flirts around Lord Boden. You know he'll stop at nothing to get what he wants. I don't suppose he expected it to be so easy, but surely you didn't think he'd leave here without winning something."

Anger flamed in Matthew's chest. He grabbed Lucinda by the arm. "What the hell are you talking about?"

She sneered. "I'm talking about the note Boden sent pretending to be you. The one left in your wife's bedchamber while you were busy dancing. I'm talking about the secret liaison to meet in that delightful summerhouse in the garden. No doubt she will be there now, believing her husband couldn't wait to kiss her again."

Panic rushed through his body like a vine, its twig-like tentacles crawling into every available space. "My footman would never have given permission for a man to go upstairs."

"Of course, Boden had a little assistance. You'd be surprised how helpful your staff can be when a lady feels unwell. But I should hurry. I fear you might already be too late."

"You're lying."

"Am I? Why don't you see for yourself? I saw Lord Boden in the garden a few minutes ago."

It couldn't be true. He would have seen Priscilla enter the ballroom unless she'd used a different entrance into the garden.

"Any lady would be shocked to find a strange man in the dark when she thought she'd be meeting her husband," Lucinda continued. "But Boden is a large man who can be very persuasive, particularly when drunk."

What option did he have? He could speak to John, race upstairs to check Priscilla was still in her chamber, but what if Lucinda was right? Boden had consumed far too much brandy, and Matthew had witnessed the look of resentment in the lord's eyes.

"I want you out of my house, Lucinda." With gritted teeth, he mumbled a curse. "I want you out of my house now. Never come here again."

An arrogant grin formed on her lips. "And what about my membership? Surely—"

"Get out of my house!" Matthew waved at Robert who was standing guard on the stairs. The footman rushed over. "Escort Miss Pearce from the premises. Ensure she has transport home. Inform Hopkins that she is no longer welcome here."

"It is of no consequence," Lucinda said, thrusting her chin in the air. "These parties used to be fun. But your wife has turned you into a dull, rather tiresome bore."

Priscilla had saved him from an empty, lonely existence. She encouraged him to be a better person.

"This world was once a fantasy. But it is a fantasy based on falsehoods. Look closely at the real people behind the masks, and you'll find it is just a horror show full of freaks."

Lucinda chuckled. "And the real horror is taking place in the summerhouse as we speak."

"You should be thankful you're not a man else you'd not be standing," he said, and then turned on his heels and raced out through the terrace doors and into the night.

CHAPTER 21

*M*atthew descended the terrace steps two at a time. Despite the lit braziers and lamps dotted around the perimeter of the garden, it was too difficult to distinguish faces in the dark. Lucinda had mentioned the summerhouse, and so he ran across the grass and darted behind the large topiary hedge.

The small wooden building sat nestled in the northwest corner of the garden. Although he'd spoken to Priscilla about auctioning the key, the room was always unlocked.

Coming to within a few feet of the tiny house, he crept up to the door. The sound of breathless pants and moans confirmed someone was inside. If Boden had touched a hair on Priscilla's head there'd be hell to pay.

Murder was the only thought on Matthew's mind when he opened the door and marched inside. Despite a red mist descending, he recognised Boden's broad frame towering over his quarry hidden in the shadows. Indeed, the guttural groans and smacking of lips awakened a rage so intense he could barely focus.

Lunging at Boden, Matthew grabbed the collar of his coat and dragged him back.

189

"What the hell?" With arms flailing Boden struggled to keep his balance as Matthew shook him like a disobedient pup.

"I've tolerated your conceit and your arrogant comments. But I warned you, lay a hand on my wife and you'll not live to see another day."

Just for good measure, and because he'd been itching to do it for weeks, Matthew released Boden and punched him hard in the stomach.

With a loud groan, the lord's head fell forward so fast his chin almost hit the floor. "What the bloody hell was that for?" Boden clutched his stomach as he tried to straighten. "I've not touched your wife. I've not seen her since … since the card game."

"You had your tongue down someone's throat."

"This is a private matter." Boden wobbled and shuffled to block the identity of the figure hiding behind the plant in the corner. "It is no concern of yours who I spend my time with."

"Who is she?" Every bone and fibre in Matthew's body told him it was not Priscilla. This lady had been a willing partner, and he trusted his wife implicitly.

"I do not have to answer to you. Why do you care?"

"Miss Pearce said you'd lured my wife out here. While I'm confident she was lying in the hope of causing me distress, I'll not leave until I learn the identity of your partner."

What was his problem? All the ladies present swopped lovers regularly.

"This is an outrage." Boden threw his hands in the air. "Can a man not have his privacy?"

"Not in my home, no." Matthew peered around Boden's shoulder. "I suggest you come out and show yourself so we can all go about our business." He glanced at Boden. "These parties are an opportunity for members to partake in illicit affairs. You have no need to fear anyone's censure."

"I fear no one," Boden spat. "And it's an affront—"

"It doesn't matter, Lawrence," the mystery figure interjected in a cool, masculine tone. "I'm certain we can be assured of Mr Chandler's discretion."

The gentleman stepped out from the shadows. His golden hair was ruffled, his lips swollen. The blush rising to his cheeks made him appear timid, angelic.

"Mr Musswell," Matthew said in as calm a voice as he could muster under the circumstances. But it wasn't anger that flowed through his veins. Indeed, seeing the look of vulnerability pass over Boden's face caused a rush of satisfaction. "Forgive me. I fear Miss Pearce likes to cause trouble. Had I not been concerned for my wife's safety, I would not have disturbed your … your evening."

"That blasted woman," Boden snapped.

Mr Musswell placed a hand on Boden's sleeve. "She has had her suspicions for some time. A woman scorned will always seek revenge."

Matthew cast his mind back a few months. He recalled talk of a liaison between Mr Musswell and Lucinda Pearce.

"Revenge is certainly on her agenda," Matthew agreed. "The lady cannot cope with rejection. She can be irrational when things don't go as she planned."

Musswell sighed. "No doubt she finds this whole situation amusing and is probably watching us from the garden."

"Oh, there is no need to worry on that score," Matthew said arrogantly. "Miss Pearce has left. I revoked her membership, told her she's not welcome in my home."

"You did what?" Boden punched the air, the strenuous activity causing him to sway and stumble. "Damn it all. God knows what she'll do now."

"Calm down, Lawrence. Anger serves no one but the Devil."

Lucinda was nothing more than a gossip, a courtesan who trampled over people to get what she wanted.

"The woman has no power over you," Matthew said. "No person in their right mind would accuse a lord of a criminal offence. If she spreads rumours, you must deny them. Indeed, it would not take much to have her refused entry to every ball and soiree."

"Mr Chandler is right, Lawrence. You give the woman too much credit."

Matthew nodded. "What you do in your personal lives is of no consequence." This was not the first time he had chanced upon a similar situation. "But may I advise that you be more discreet in future. Conducting a liaison so openly is courting trouble."

"It's that bloody brandy," Boden cried. "I am normally a man in complete control of my urges."

Matthew shrugged. "Perhaps you should have had the port. It was a particularly good bottle. Indeed, my wife had a new decanter brought in just before the game."

Boden's eyes widened. "Yes … yes. Perhaps you're right."

"Indeed, I find brandy affects one's facial expressions. You appeared to develop a twitch before playing a knave. An excessively arched brow equated to a queen."

Boden's face turned beetroot red. He mumbled and stuttered but couldn't form a coherent word.

"Are you all right, Lawrence?" Musswell enquired. "Are you ill? Is it the brandy?"

"Now, I shall leave you gentlemen to your business." Matthew tugged at the sleeves of his coat and brushed imagined dust from his lapels. "I hope to see you tomorrow, Lord Boden. I shall look forward to ripping up my vowel and watching it burn. When you play cards again, you should refrain from drinking brandy. Twitches are often mistaken for silent communication, and I'm certain you would hate for others to think you a cheat." Matthew inclined his head. "Good evening, gentlemen."

With a grin stretching from ear to ear, Matthew left them to their affairs. He had taken but two strides across the lawn when he heard Boden's frustrated curses rent the air. While annoyed with

Lucinda for causing mischief, finding Boden in a clinch with a male lover was a fitting reward.

Matthew was still smiling to himself when he entered the ballroom, but Robert's frantic gesture from his position on the stairs banished all amusing thoughts. Perhaps Lucinda refused to leave and was intent on making a scene.

Matthew strode over. "What is it, Robert? Please tell me you got rid of her."

"No, the … the lady, sir. She's had an accident, tripped and tumbled on her way out. She hit her head hard on the front steps."

Bloody hell!

"All I asked you to do was escort her to the damn door." This was probably another one of Lucinda's games to get attention. "I assume we're talking of Miss Pearce?"

Robert nodded. "Hopkins came looking but couldn't find you."

"I trust she's not dead." Matthew accompanied the footman out into the hall. Relief filled his chest when he saw John standing to attention at the bottom of the stairs.

"No, sir. She's in the drawing room. We carried her and laid her out on the chaise."

"But she is breathing?"

Robert nodded again. "She looks to be sleeping."

"Take me to her." He had no desire to be alone in a room with the vixen.

Hopkins appeared behind them, his breathless pants audible. "Sir, has … has Robert—"

"Yes, yes. I know about Miss Pearce. Follow me, Hopkins."

They all marched into the drawing room, stood on the rug in the centre, shocked to find no sign of the injured Miss Pearce.

"Where the hell is she?" Matthew stabbed his finger at the empty chaise. "Where the hell has she gone?"

"But I don't understand." Robert scratched his head. "She was here a few minutes ago."

With his heart pounding hard in his chest, Matthew scanned the room. "Well, she's not here now." He strode over to the window and searched behind the drapes, noticed the slight breeze coming from the gap between the sash and the ledge. Surely she'd not climbed out of the window? "Why the blazes did you leave her alone?"

You'd be surprised how helpful your staff can be when a lady feels unwell.

Miss Pearce's words had come back to haunt him.

"Perhaps she felt better, sir, and wandered back to the ballroom."

"Then let us go and speak to John."

They returned to the hall.

"After Robert and Hopkins carried Miss Pearce to the drawing room, at any point did she return to the hall?"

"No, sir. Other than Mr Chigwell and Mrs Wilson, I've seen no one else."

Hopkins cleared his throat. "I was in the ballroom at the time, sir. It was John and Robert who carried Miss Pearce into the room and made her comfortable."

Matthew blinked and shook his head, somehow hoping it would solve the problem with his hearing. He shot around to face John. "Are you telling me you left the stairs unattended?"

The colour drained from John's face until his pallor was ashen, an odd shade of grey. "Just for a moment. Miss Pearce injured her head. We couldn't wake her. I … I couldn't leave her lying on the steps. Robert struggled to carry her on his own."

"Bloody hell!"

It was as though a hundred needles pierced his heart. He'd underestimated Lucinda's skill for deception. All the signs had been there. Matthew pushed the footman aside.

Fists clenched he mounted the stairs, fearing what he would find.

CHAPTER 22

*T*he sight of frantic couples darting around the garden like ghosts in the night, searching for an available place to conduct a liaison, gave Priscilla faith in Matthew's ability to empty the house early.

She stood at the window, her palm pressed against the cold pane, waiting to catch a glimpse of her husband rounding up the rabble. Just the sight of him made her feel warm inside. Happy. Complete.

Love was like a sweet form of agony.

Whenever she thought about him her heart swelled so large it filled her chest. Her body tingled in his presence. She yearned for his company. Hungered for his kisses. Craved his touch.

A whimper left her lips.

He felt something, too. Only time would tell if the flashes of emotion she noted in his eyes would develop into something more profound. But she could wait.

In her moment of contemplation, her thoughts drifted back to the card game. The rush of satisfaction, the pure sense of exhilaration when they'd beaten Lord Boden was like nothing she'd ever experienced before. It had nothing to do with winning back the vowel, with revenge or a desire to see the arrogance wiped from Boden's face.

Matthew's triumphant grin, his puffed chest and square shoulders, the confidence oozing from his pores, was worth the trauma of playing a dozen tense games.

The creak of the connecting door opening in the dressing room disturbed her reverie. From the ravenous look in Matthew's eye when he'd left her on the stairs, she suspected he could not wait two hours without partaking in a little amorous activity.

Fighting the urge to run into his embrace, Priscilla continued to stare out of the window. The smile on her lips stretched wide as she anticipated strong arms sliding around her waist, the feel of his arousal pressed against her buttocks.

God, her throat grew tight.

The light padding of steps towards her made her heart beat so fast she could barely catch her breath. Soon … soon she would feel his hot lips against her neck.

With her mind lost in a heady cloud of desire, she closed her eyes and inhaled. Matthew's unique scent always found a way to seep into her skin, to awaken every fibre of her being, to—

Her eyes flew open.

The smell of stale tobacco, a rank whiff of liquor, the fusty scent of days-old sweat clawed at her nostrils and bombarded her senses.

Panic flared.

She clutched her hands to her chest to stop her body shaking. Amidst the warm glow of candlelight, she saw him then, caught a fleeting glimpse reflected in the glass. His round face and swollen cheeks reminded her of a squirrel carrying food for winter. While Matthew was muscular yet lean, this man's rotund physique filled her frame of vision.

Every second spent thinking brought him closer.

Had he honest intentions in mind, he would have coughed to gain her attention, introduced himself for fear of startling her. There was little point knocking the window. The guests were engaged in their usual antics, and would never hear the rapping above their grunts and groans.

With no other choice left open, Priscilla swung around.

It took a moment for her mind to confirm the gentleman's identity. "Mr Mullworth," she said, feigning the confidence of a duchess. "What on earth are you doing in my private chamber? Are you lost? Did Mr Chandler give you permission to enter his room?"

One after another, the questions tumbled out of her mouth. Talking settled her nerves.

"There is no need to be coy, my dear. Miss Pearce gave me your note." Mullworth stepped closer. "You said to come through the master suite to avoid detection."

Heaven help her. What was she to do?

"I'm surprised you managed to sneak past the footman."

"Miss Pearce created a little diversion." Mullworth's greedy gaze fell to the jewelled brooch on her bodice. The tip of his tongue moistened the seam of his lips. "Of course, the woman has her own agenda. I'm sure you're aware of her obsession with your husband. But let's not talk about that now. Time is of the essence."

As Mullworth took another step, Priscilla knew she had to move away from the window if she had any hope of escaping.

"If you have come here expecting something from me, then I'm afraid you'll be disappointed." Taking a few discreet side-steps for fear of him pouncing, she shuffled into the middle of the room. "Surely after witnessing the way I danced with my husband, you must know there has been a mistake. Is it not obvious I am in love with him?"

Mullworth's frown was quickly replaced with a sly grin. "As

your note said, that is the game you play to make the gentlemen try harder to win your affection."

Good Lord, with her talent for deception, Miss Pearce should work for the Crown.

Priscilla edged closer to the door. "Miss Pearce is the one playing games, sir. She will use any tactic necessary to get my husband's attention."

"What are you saying?" Mullworth's fleshy jowls wobbled.

"There has been a misunderstanding. I will never engage in any activity unless it's with my husband."

A moment of silence ensued while the gentleman scrutinised her face.

"Ah, I understand," he said, his straggly eyebrows wiggling up and down. "You wish for the three of us to partake in a liaison together. I mean it's not what I'm used to, and I'm not sure what Chandler will—"

"For heaven's sake, no! Does anyone in this house possess a rational mind?" Priscilla sucked in a breath and thrust her arm out towards the door. "I suggest you leave, sir, before my husband finds you in here and blows a hole in the middle of your forehead."

Surely the thought of a dawn appointment would make the man reconsider his position. But no. The faint chime of the long-case clock in the hall sent the man into a mild panic.

With hands flapping, Mullworth closed the gap between them. "Come on now. You're married to Chandler. A little wild sport with the guests is expected."

"How many times must I tell you? I shall sleep with no man other than my husband."

Fat, chapped fingers gripped her shoulder. His head fell forward as he ogled her breasts. Priscilla stepped back, but his grip was firm.

"One kiss, just to see if you like it." Mullworth puckered his lips which brought relief from his repugnant breath. Both hands settled on her shoulders. "Just one before it's time to leave."

Priscilla struggled to raise her arms. She kicked out, but the man was too drunk to care.

"Come on," he continued as she turned her head away to avoid his kiss. "Chandler won't object. The guests' needs always come first."

"Let me go, Mr Mullworth, or I'll scream."

A growl resonated from the back of his throat. "You'll kiss me, woman, else I shall withdraw my membership."

"Consider it done." Matthew's deep, masculine roar filled the room. "Right after I've knocked your damn teeth down your throat. Now, get your filthy hands off my wife."

Relief coursed through Priscilla's veins. As soon as Mullworth released her, she sagged to the floor.

Mullworth swung around and raised his hands as a shield. "There's no need for violence, Chandler."

"Oh, there's every need." Matthew took a step forward. He had the air of the Devil: dark, menacing, utterly terrifying.

Priscilla shuffled back.

"I thought the chit was interested. A fellow can't help it if he's misread the signs."

"Course not." Matthew crossed the room in a few strides. "Just so there can be no confusion in future, let this act as a reminder." With a few short, sharp jabs, Matthew punched Mr Mullworth in the stomach. The man's shrill cries filled the room. He reeled, staggering back a few steps. "And maybe one more in case your memory fails you." One uppercut to the chin sent Mr Mullworth up into the air, and he landed with a thud.

Priscilla gasped.

Matthew marched to the bedchamber door, turned the key in the lock, yanked it open and stomped out onto the landing. "John," he shouted over the balustrade. "Come up here and get this good-for-nothing piece of *shite* out of my home."

Within seconds, John and Hopkins appeared at her door. Both men entered the room, their frantic gazes focusing on the lifeless lump. The butler's face turned ashen when he noticed her crouched on the floor.

"Forgive me, madam." Hopkins inclined his head. "Our task was to protect you, and we have failed."

"It's all right, Hopkins. There's no harm done." The tremble in her voice said otherwise.

John's face flushed, and he pursed his lips. "It's my fault, madam. I left my post."

Matthew sighed and thrust his hand through his hair. "It is no one's fault but mine." He shook his head, though struggled to look at her. "Now, throw this oaf into his carriage. Inform his coachman that if I see him within a hundred yards of my home, there'll be hell to pay."

The servants nodded, heaved Mr Mullworth to his feet, took an arm each and carried him out.

Matthew followed them onto the landing. "Find Lawson and Pike. I want everyone out of the house. Check the summerhouse and scour the garden. Give me a few minutes, and I'll be down to help. Follow the procedure we use in case of a fire. That should prevent any arguments."

The men's mumbled replies were barely audible through the din below.

Expressing a weary sigh, Matthew returned to the room and closed the door.

For a few seconds he stood there and stared at her, his mouth drawn into a thin, sombre line. What she regarded as sparkling emerald eyes were now the colour of the sea on a dull overcast day.

"I'm sorry." The words breezed from his lips on a whisper.

Priscilla stood. "You weren't to know."

It was as though they were standing on opposite sides of a

valley, the space between them vast, growing wider by the minute.

The gaunt, haunted look in his eyes marred his handsome face. "When I saw him in here … when I …"

She took a step towards him and held out her hands. The gesture caused him to suck in a breath, and he crossed the room and pulled her into an embrace.

"I'm sorry, Priscilla." Large hands stroked her hair, patted her back and shoulders as though searching for a sign of a wound or injury. "What was I thinking? What husband would allow his wife to live in these conditions?"

Priscilla pulled back and touched his cheek. "Don't blame yourself. A wife was not on your agenda when you planned these parties. These things cannot be helped. Next time—"

"There won't be a next time." He covered her hand, brought it to his lips and kissed it five times or more. "One's home should be a place of solace, a place of safety. To hell with the lot of them. Let them find their entertainment elsewhere. I'll find some other way to supplement my income. Lord, we can take to the gaming hells if we get desperate."

Priscilla managed a smile. The event with Mr Mullworth had left her shaken. "I'm not worried, and so you shouldn't be."

He nodded. "Together we will find a way to muddle through."

"We'll do better than that. You'll spend your days painting, your nights in bed pleasing me. I shall spend my days organising your diary, entertaining patrons and raising our children. Every night I shall show you how much I love you."

She waited for the flash of fear in his eyes at the mere mention of children and love. But it never came.

"It sounds perfect," he said, offering a wide grin. "But you omitted to mention one vital part."

"Oh, and what is that?"

He opened his mouth, but no words followed. His watery eyes glistened in the candlelight.

Doubt surfaced and her bottom lip trembled. "We promised to be honest, remember. If I've been presumptuous or made an error—"

"No. As always your words speak of nothing but the truth. But there is something else I intend to do as well as painting and rousing your exquisite cries upon release."

The muscles in her core pulsed whenever he mentioned anything amorous.

He cupped her face between his large hands and kissed her softly on the lips. "I intend to love you my whole life."

"Love me?" The world seemed to tilt on its axis and she fought to keep her balance. "But are you not a man incapable of deep affection?"

The corner of his mouth curled up. "Only where other people are concerned. But I love you, Priscilla, with every fibre of my being."

A well of suppressed emotion burst. A tear trickled down her cheek. She couldn't help it. Indeed, she was in danger of becoming a blubbering wreck.

"Don't cry." He brushed the tear away with the pad of his thumb. "Are you not happy to hear my declaration?"

"My lack of confidence begs that I challenge you, but you would not have spoken the words unless you meant them."

"I would never lie to you, and I am not a man who says things just to please other people." He brushed his mouth against hers, the kiss sweet, tender. "Damn. I must be in love with you as the thought of holding you close whilst still fully clothed seems appealing."

"What, you don't want to bed me?"

"Of course I want to bed you. Trust me. I could rouse the required response within seconds. But holding you in my arms is fulfilling. Just being near you soothes my soul."

She did cry then, a fast-flowing river that carried away all her fears and doubts.

Matthew held her to his chest, stroked her back and whispered endearments.

Sucking in a breath, she raised her head to look at him. "If the dowager Lady Morford were here I think I'd kiss her."

"Indeed. When I agreed to marry you, I thought I had settled my debt to Tristan." The warm glow of candlelight danced over his handsome features. "Now it is evident I owe him a far greater debt, one that can never be repaid."

A feeling of contentment filled her breast. "Dance with me."

"Dance? But there's no music."

"I can hear love's melody."

Matthew smiled. "Are we to move fast or slow?"

"Slow. I want to savour the moment."

He held her close, hummed a sweet tune as they moved in perpetual circles around the room. Priscilla placed her head on his chest, inhaled the unique scent that made her knees weak.

"I love you," he whispered into her hair.

"I love you."

They tried to ignore the loud rap on the door, but the caller grew more persistent.

"We should answer it," he said as they came to a halt. "No doubt there is trouble downstairs. And the sooner we get rid of them, the sooner we can enjoy the rest of the evening."

The thought of joining him in bed sent shocks of desire shooting to her core. "Then what are you waiting for?"

He chuckled, marched over to the door and yanked it open. "What is it, Hopkins?"

"Forgive me, sir," Hopkins said.

"Are the drunken fools refusing to leave? Did you not ring the damn handbell?"

"If you don't come down, fists will be flying. Lawson is at the end of his tether, and I fear he's liable to do some lord harm and hang for the privilege."

"Bloody hell." Matthew pushed his hand through his hair. He

turned to face her. "I should go down. Lock the door behind me, and the one in the dressing room, too."

"Mr Mullworth regained consciousness when we loaded him into the carriage," Hopkins added. "He asked me to convey his apologies."

"The bastard can go to hell," Matthew snapped.

Hopkins inclined his head. "That's what I told him, sir. Oh, and Lord Boden said to tell you he intends to make sure Miss Pearce leaves for France on the first available crossing."

Priscilla breathed a sigh of relief. The woman was intent on causing trouble. "Thank goodness, although it beggars the question why Lord Boden would want to help us."

A sly grin touched Matthew's lips. "When I come back, remind me to tell you about Lord Boden's new hobby."

Curiosity flared. "You can't leave without giving me a clue."

"Let us just say that Boden's wants and desires are not as straightforward as they seem. I shall leave you to ponder the comment."

A string of vile curses echoed up the stairs.

Hopkins rushed to look over the balustrade. "Damn it, Pike. Put the man down and let him walk out."

Priscilla rushed to Matthew's side. "Go, before all the staff find themselves dangling from the hangman's noose."

He kissed her roughly on the lips. "Lock the door." He took two steps forward, hurried back to her side and kissed her again. "Have I told you I love you?"

Priscilla smiled. "Three times."

"I promise to say it at least another ten times before the night is out." Without another word, he raced down the stairs.

"What's going on, Chandler?" a loud voice rumbled from the hallway. "Is there a fire?"

Priscilla closed the door and turned the key. She touched her forehead to the wooden panel, closed her eyes and let happiness consume her.

Matthew loved her.

The stranger who'd rescued her in the garden had become her life, her love, her everything.

The future held nothing but promise.

EPILOGUE

*W*ith the room painted a dark shade of red and an abundance of gilt-framed canvases littering the walls, the picture gallery was unrecognisable from the ballroom once used to entertain the dissolute members of the *ton*.

Matthew sat on one of the circular velvet seats positioned in the centre and stared up at the large rectangular portrait of Priscilla. He had captured her likeness to perfection, even if he did say so himself. The innocence of porcelain skin, golden hair and angelic blue eyes were counterbalanced by full sinful lips.

The red dress she wore reminded him of the night she'd first found the courage to wander downstairs with the sole objective of seducing him. While she remembered the night for that reason, in truth, she had enticed him long before. He'd just been too blind to realise.

A smile formed on his lips as his gaze lingered on the curve of her breast visible above the bodice of her gown. This painting was for public viewing. Hidden in his chamber, he had a much smaller version. One purely for personal pleasure. Of course, artists were rarely happy with their work and were forever making changes and alterations. Even after twenty or so sittings, he just couldn't seem to master the soft swell of her breasts or flare of her hips.

"There you are." Priscilla's voice disturbed his reverie.

Matthew glanced up. Priscilla was attempting to navigate the stairs, but with her stomach swollen with their child, she struggled to see where to place her feet.

"Let me help you." He jumped up and rushed to offer his assistance.

She gripped his hand and descended the five small steps. "You seemed lost in thought. Are you still finding fault with your work or were you dreaming about me?"

"Both, though it's the portrait in my chamber that needs some adjustments."

"Didn't you put the finishing touches to it last week?" she said, eyeing him with some suspicion.

His gaze fell to her full breasts filling the bodice. "I fear there is a little more of you since then."

She stroked her stomach. "Oh, Matthew. You can't paint my portrait when I look like this."

"Why? You look beautiful, and at the moment, you can't seem to get enough of me."

A blush touched her cheeks. "I have the same problem with food."

"Well, you may devour me whenever the mood takes you."

She arched a mischievous brow. "If we weren't expecting guests I might find something to nibble on now."

"Nibble? The word is hardly flattering and implies I'm lacking in that department."

"I have never found you lacking in any department." With a satisfied smile, she glanced around the room. "The paintings look far more impressive when displayed properly."

"You mean instead of hiding in a dusty attic." A sudden pang of self-doubt hit him square in the chest. "What if no one comes?"

She jerked her head back. "Of course people will come. I

dealt with the invitations myself. Uncle Herbert has made it his mission to fill the room. Indeed, three people are interested in purchasing *Lost in the Forest* and have started a bidding war. And the Marquess of Danesfield wants to commission you to paint a portrait of his wife. He has come to town to visit Tristan's friend, Mr Danbury."

To have the marquess as a patron would increase the value of his work considerably.

"You know Lord Boden came to see me yesterday. He offered me a thousand pounds to paint Mr Musswell. The extortionate fee is to buy my discretion, of course."

"A thousand pounds," she gasped. "Can he afford such a sum? He hasn't gambled since they found Mr Travant's body floating in the Thames."

"Boden said Travant owed money to a man in Seven Dials and tried to leave the country without paying. I think Boden feared a similar fate. If we worked out his signs and signals, someone else was bound to."

Priscilla nodded. "I trust Mr Musswell is to have his clothes on when you paint his likeness."

Matthew had not even thought to ask the question. "Should he require a more *Adamesque* portrayal, you'll have to act as my chaperone. With our child on the way, I'll not turn down the offer of a thousand pounds."

"Well, I've seen enough bare behinds not to have a fear of them."

"Seeing them from the window and seeing them in the flesh is vastly different." He chuckled.

The smile on Priscilla's face faded as she searched his face. "Do your fears stem purely from the fact people might not like your work? Or is something else troubling you?"

Priscilla was adept at reading his mind. As she'd asked direct questions, he could not lie to her.

He opened his mouth to speak but struggled to find the right words.

Priscilla held his hand. "Is it the fact your brother is accompanying Uncle Herbert?"

Damn. Would seeing his brother rouse all the old feelings of resentment? Did he have it in his heart to forgive?

"What the hell will I say to him?" Matthew clutched her hand tight. "What if I feel nothing but hatred in my heart?"

"You won't. Your heart is full of love. Since your mother's passing, Simon has tried to reach out to you. Be the better person and accept his hand with good grace."

With Priscilla at his side, anything seemed possible.

He sighed. "No doubt Simon will be just as apprehensive."

"I promise you, all will be well," she said, and he believed her.

Hopkins appeared at the top of the stairs. "Lord and Lady Morford have arrived, sir."

"Show them in, Hopkins." Matthew had asked Tristan to come an hour early purely to help banish the nerves. But the sight of the couple only made the event of the day seem all the more real.

The Morfords had barely reached the bottom step when Pricilla came forward, took Isabella's hands and held them tight.

"Oh, I'm so glad you're here." Priscilla glanced down at Isabella's swollen stomach with a look of camaraderie. "Matthew is tired of hearing me talk of cribs and christening gowns."

Isabella smiled and appeared just as eager to talk of their shared experiences. "Then let us leave the gentlemen to their business while we sit and converse over tea."

Their wives kissed them on the cheek, assisted each other up the stairs and hurried from the room.

"I hope you don't mind, but I invited Marcus and Anna along," Tristan said. "They're in London for a few weeks, and I want you to meet them."

"Not at all. The more people seen admiring my work, the more appealing my paintings will seem. But I thought the Danburys preferred to stay in France."

"They do. After her own harrowing experience, Anna wanted to open an agency in London for ladies of quality who find themselves on hard times. She is interviewing people for the post of manager."

"An agency? It all sounds rather intriguing."

"The idea is to provide board and lodgings while the ladies find their way in the world. She hopes to help with employment and education, too."

"When I hear of such altruistic pursuits, I can't help but be ashamed of the years I wasted on the dissolute."

"Trust me." Tristan patted Matthew on the back. "We've all done things we'd rather forget. The important thing is what we do with our time now."

Matthew glanced around the room. A deep sense of pride filled his chest when he considered what he'd achieved. "It's hard to imagine this was once a place where drunken lords gobbled grapes from a lady's cleavage. Where people frolicked openly with their lovers."

"I can hardly believe it's the same room." Tristan scanned the walls with a look of wonder. "By God, if I'd known you were this talented I'd never have let you waste time hosting lewd parties."

The compliment touched him.

"Had it not been for Priscilla, the paintings would still be locked away in the attic." He clutched Tristan's shoulder. "Can you imagine what my life would be like had I not offered my assistance that night in Holbrook's garden?"

Tristan grabbed Matthew's forearm. "Can you imagine what all our lives would be like had you not found the courage to marry?"

They both shivered visibly.

"Let's not think of it," Matthew said, feeling a slight bout of nausea at the prospect. The thought of never burying himself inside his wife's welcoming body, the thought of never having experienced the depths of true love, terrified him. "Let us count ourselves amongst the luckiest of men."

"Indeed," Tristan said with a burst of optimism. "Through our shared experiences we have proven to be men willing to fight for a cause."

"We have proven we are men who would do anything for love."

THE END

Thank you for reading ***What You Promised.***

If you enjoyed this book, please consider leaving a review at the online bookseller of your choice.

∼

Discover more about the author at
www.adeleclee.com

∼

Turn the page if you would like to read an excerpt from

The Mysterious Miss Flint

Book 1 in the Lost Ladies of London series

THE MYSTERIOUS MISS FLINT

LOST LADIES OF LONDON BOOK 1

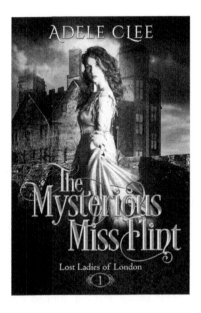

The earl's goal was to find his missing sister.

The last thing he expected to find was love.

THE MYSTERIOUS MISS FLINT

CHAPTER 1

"What the hell do you mean? You must know where she is." Oliver Darby, fourth Earl of Stanton, rounded the solid oak desk, grabbed the solicitor by the flimsy lapels of his coat and shook him. "Wickedness is in the blood. My father is dead and buried, but I am very much alive. Now tell me where he sent her."

"The … the late earl made no mention of it in his will, my lord." The man's neat white periwig slipped down to cover one eye. "Perhaps Lady Rose went to stay with an aunt."

"Lies, I can deal with. Stupidity, I cannot." Oliver released the pathetic creature, and he tumbled back into the chair. "We have no other kin, and you damn well know it."

Mr Wild straightened his wig. "What about your sister's godmother, Lady Stewart?"

"Neither of us have seen Lady Stewart since our mother died. Our father forbade any contact." Oliver's tone conveyed more than contempt for his father's controlling manner. "And according to the housekeeper, no one has seen my sister for six months or more. I think that's a little long for a visit, don't you?"

"My lord, I don't know what else to suggest." Mr Wild

winced as though expecting another volatile outburst. "I assume you have questioned the staff."

Questioned them? Oliver had torn the house apart to find answers.

He'd interrogated the servants until they confessed to all manner of misdemeanours. The footman's dalliance with the maid was hardly surprising. The housekeeper's deception over the price of a bottle of brandy proved more so. Mrs Baker's brother was the proprietor of a liquor establishment. Any extra funds gained from the forged bills were passed to the housekeeper to purchase candles, since his father had reduced the household budget.

Despite hours of prodding and probing, none of the servants knew what had happened to Rose. Most presumed she was visiting friends in the country even though she'd left without her maid.

A sense of foreboding gripped him.

"I want a detailed breakdown of my father's … of *my* assets," Oliver corrected. "A list of all land owned regardless of how small the plot." An image of a shallow grave entered his mind, and he cursed under his breath. Surely the bastard wasn't cruel enough to do away with his own daughter simply to spite his rebellious son? "I want a list of all property owned outright, and any bought in partnership. Include all buildings rented by tenants."

Had rational thought abandoned him?

Perhaps Rose had eloped and decided to break all contact with her family. Based on their father's possessive nature no one would blame her. Perhaps she would breeze into the dining room this evening with rosy cheeks and a bright smile and regale him with tales of time spent in Brighton.

The painful knot in his stomach said otherwise. Rose had failed to attend the funeral, failed to appear to hear the solicitor read the will.

Mr Wild coughed. "I'm afraid I have a three o'clock appointment, my lord, and couldn't possibly assist you today. But I can prepare the papers tomorrow."

"Tomorrow!" An innocent young woman was missing. And it was Oliver's fault for leaving her in the care of a brute. Panic came in the form of a hard lump in his throat. "You'll give me what I want now else I'll empty every damn drawer myself."

Mr Wild loosened the collar of his shirt and fanned his face. "My lord—"

"Now, Mr Wild!"

The man stood, though there was doubt as to whether his legs would support his weight. He scurried out into the hall and called Mr Andrews, the clerk.

While the two men ferreted about in drawers and cabinets, piling papers and files on top of the desk, Oliver contemplated the part he'd played in neglecting his sister.

The day his father insisted he marry Lady Melissa Martin, the most arrogant, conceited debutante ever to grace a ballroom, was the day he left Stanton House and the fog-drenched streets of London behind. His escape took him as far afield as Naples until his father cut him off without a penny. But Oliver was nothing if not resourceful. He'd always excelled at cards and had stumbled upon many a wealthy, drunken sot eager to part with his purse.

"I think that's the lot." Mr Andrews pushed his spectacles up to the bridge of his nose. "Do you need any further assistance, Mr Wild?"

"No, Andrews, that will be all."

"Wait." Oliver gestured to the mountain of paper. "I want a single list of all land and property. If Mr Wild has no objection, you may take notes." Oliver raised a brow and stared down his nose at the agitated solicitor. "And lock the front door. Unfortunately, Mr Wild cannot make his three o'clock appointment."

Arrogance was a trait Oliver despised. As was using one's position to control and manipulate people. But Rose was missing, hidden away in some godforsaken place so his father could punish him from beyond the grave.

Mr Wild offered no objection to the demands made. Yet the hint of disdain about his countenance mirrored the look Oliver had cast his father many times in the past.

A pang of remorse for his high-handed approach hit him squarely in the chest. "Had my father's man of business not disappeared along with half the silver, I would have had him attend to this sorry task."

"Mr Burrows did not disappear," Mr Wild said, brushing the dust from his hands. "Your father dismissed him some time before his death. Burrows had not been paid for six months, and no doubt thought to take the cutlery to pay his rent."

"Why? My father was not short of funds." On the contrary, Oliver had inherited a substantial income. Regardless of his father's disapproval and their subsequent estrangement, continuing the Darby bloodline was paramount—the only thing that mattered.

But it took more than money to produce offspring worthy of a life of privilege and title. It took marriage to a simpering debutante from good stock. It meant conforming to the rigid rules Oliver had fought long and hard to avoid. Witnessing his parents' constant battles was enough to convince any man of the merits of bachelorhood. Indeed, the only promise he'd made was that the Darby line ended with him.

"From what I gather, they were at odds over business." Mr Wild sat in the chair behind the desk and opened the first file. "The refusal to pay Burrows was simply an act of defiance."

Oliver gave a snort of contempt as he dropped into the seat opposite. "My father liked to make a point."

Mr Wild's resigned nod spoke of personal experience. "So, other than Stanton House and Bridewell, there's the shooting lodge on Loch Broom." He turned to his clerk. "Are you writing this down, Andrews?"

The clerk nodded from the small desk in the corner of the room.

"There's the house on St James' Street," Wild continued, flicking through the documents, "one on Mount Street and the house bequeathed to your late mother in Acton, Shropshire."

Scotland! Shropshire! The list went on.

Bloody hell!

He'd been the earl for almost a week, missed the funeral but had made it home for the reading of the will. In light of Rose's disappearance, the finer details had seemed unimportant. Hearing the vast extent of his father's estate filled Oliver with dread. Despite searching Bridewell—their family seat in Sussex—and finding nothing, the accompanying eight thousand acres would take months to search.

The more the list grew, the more Oliver's temple throbbed. All the other houses mentioned were leased to tenants. It would mean investigating every one—a mammoth task for a man on his own. And while he plodded about from one county to the next, heaven knows what predicament Rose found herself in.

"What about derelict buildings?" Oliver said, his tone more subdued now.

Various images flashed into his mind. A damp rat-infested cellar. A crumbling shelter, home to stray dogs and vagabonds.

Mr Wild frowned. "Your father would not have sent Lady Rose to a place unbefitting her station."

Oh, his father would have sent them both to the devil.

Thankfully, Oliver possessed the Darby family traits: slightly crooked little fingers, a V-shaped hairline and a Roman nose with an aristocratic bump on the bridge. The Darbys were ugly men. However, Oliver had been fortunate enough to inherit his mother's striking blue eyes, full lips and evenly spaced features. The old earl's obsession with his wife's beauty led to suspicions of infidelity and was the cause of his distant relationship with Rose. While Oliver had hair as black as his father's soul, Rose was the only Darby ever to possess honey-gold tresses.

But to send her away, to ignore her absence and pretend she'd never existed.

"My father would go to any lengths necessary to achieve his goal." Numerous times he had demanded Oliver return home. Had Oliver known Rose was to be a pawn in their game, he would have employed different tactics.

"The list is extensive," Mr Wild said as he tied the string around the last file and placed it with the others. "Perhaps an enquiry agent might help you to investigate those properties further afield. If you plan to search the length and breadth of the country yourself, may I suggest you start at Gretna Green."

"I shall consider my options." Oliver wouldn't rest until he'd checked every property, although hiring an agent in Scotland might save him weeks of unnecessary hours on the road.

"A gentleman of your status and position requires someone to manage his investments. Should you need such a man, I am happy to make a recommendation."

Deception was rife, it appeared. Oliver trusted no one. "I prefer to keep my own accounts for the time being."

"As you wish." Wild pulled his watch from his waistcoat pocket and checked the time. "And does that conclude our business for today, my lord?"

"It does," Oliver replied as the clerk approached the desk and handed him the written list of assets. His stomach churned at the thought of the monumental task ahead. "And you're certain that's everything?"

"Indeed." Wild gripped the arms of his chair and edged forward, a manoeuvre to encourage Oliver to stand.

While sitting in the confines of the small, musty office, the job of finding his sister seemed achievable. Everything he needed was on the single piece of paper in his hand. Hope blossomed in his chest if only for a fleeting moment.

But the world was a vast place when someone was missing.

The clerk's persistent cough and constant shuffling dragged Oliver from his reverie.

"What is it, Andrews?" Mr Wild said, his gritted teeth masked by a forced smile.

"It's just that the late earl also did business with Mr Jameson." The clerk shrank back as soon as the words left his mouth.

"Jameson? But that's ridiculous. I was the earl's solicitor." Wild scowled. "What need had he to visit with Mr Jameson?"

The clerk's mouth curled downwards. "Perhaps it was a personal matter, sir."

"But I dealt with all matters. You must be mistaken, Andrews."

Oliver exhaled. "Can we not simply call Mr Jameson in and ask him?"

Mr Andrews took a hesitant step forward. "Mr Jameson is away at Park Hall, drawing up papers for Viscount Trench."

"In that case, he can offer no objection. Find my father's file and bring it here."

Both men looked at him as though he'd suggested sacrificing all first-born males.

Mr Wild shook his head. "We cannot enter a colleague's office without his permission. We must wait for him to return."

"If your colleague drew up papers for my father, then they belong to me. The fact Jameson has failed to pass them over to you is suspicious, is it not?"

There was a prolonged silence.

"Very well." Oliver shot to his feet. "I shall search for the file myself."

"No, no." Mr Wild waved his hands in the air as he scanned the breadth of Oliver's chest. "It is best that I go. The drawers are full of private documents. Should our clients learn of a security breach they may take their business elsewhere."

Oliver gestured to the door. "Then let's get to it." There wasn't a minute to waste.

Accompanied by the clerk, they entered the office across the hall from Mr Wild's. The room was just as dark and dingy. Breathing the musty air was akin to sucking in sawdust.

Wild scurried over to a tall cabinet, glanced back over his shoulder numerous times as if expecting Jameson to jump out from behind the coat stand.

"This is highly irregular," Wild muttered as he flicked through the contents of a drawer. "I can see nothing listed under Stanton or Darby."

"Then I suggest you look again." An odd feeling in the pit of Oliver's stomach convinced him they were looking in the right place. "See if there's a file under the name of Benting."

Mr Benting was an alias used by his father when he wished to travel incognito. When he stalked his wife and booked into coaching inns to check she wasn't meeting a lover.

Wild opened another drawer and scanned the row of files. "Yes, there is a Benting," he said with some surprise. He placed the thin file on Mr Jameson's cluttered desk, read a missive, and then examined a document embossed with a wax seal.

"Well?" Oliver's fingers tingled as he contemplated ripping the document out from under the solicitor's nose. "What have you found?"

"There is no proof that the Mr Benting mentioned here is your father. There is nothing to suggest a connection or why he purchased the property." Wild glanced down at the piece of paper and shook his head. "Without Mr Jameson to corroborate Andrews' story, I'm afraid there is nothing more I can tell you."

Even if Mr Jameson were available, he would have received a substantial reward to keep his tongue.

"Indeed," Wild continued, "I fear there has been a terrible misunderstanding."

A misunderstanding? The comment caused an irritating prickle at Oliver's nape.

"You mentioned a property," Oliver said, his curiosity piqued. There had to be a reason why his father was secretive about the purchase. "Can you not tell me where it is? Is anyone living there?"

"Such places are never short of occupants," Wild answered cryptically. "But it appears there is some mistake. The property was bequeathed to a Miss Flint, although she has yet to come forward and claim her inheritance."

Who the hell was Miss Flint?

"Then I see no harm in riding there and introducing myself." Perhaps his father's jealousy stemmed from guilt. Could Miss Flint be his father's mistress? To discover the old earl was a hypocrite would be amusing under less dire circumstances.

The solicitor's eyes glazed over. "Good Lord, the manor is not somewhere one visits whilst in the neighbourhood. I cannot imagine why anyone would want to stop at such a place."

"Really? Why ever not?"

"Because Morton Manor is an asylum."

Printed in Great Britain
by Amazon

22364855R00128